DOUBLEDAY
CELEBRATES
100 YEARS OF
EXCELLENCE

Pure
Slaughter
Value

Robert
Bingham

Doubleday

New York | London | Toronto | Sydney | Auckland

PUBLISHED BY DOUBLEDAY
a division of Bantam Doubleday Dell Publishing Group, Inc.
1540 Broadway, New York, New York 10036

DOUBLEDAY and the portrayal of an anchor with a dolphin
are trademarks of Doubleday, a division of
Bantam Doubleday Dell Publishing Group, Inc.

Book design by Debbie Glasserman

These stories are works of fiction. Names, characters, places,
and incidents either are the product of the author's imagina-
tion or are used fictitiously. Any resemblance to actual per-
sons, living or dead, events, or locales is entirely coincidental.
Some of the stories in this collection have appeared, in slightly
different form, in the following publications: "The Other
Family" and "The Target Audience" in *The New Yorker* and
"Bad Stars" in *Might*.

Library of Congress Cataloging-in-Publication Data

Bingham, Robert.
Pure Slaughter value.
p.   cm.
PS3552.I496P8   1997
813'.54—dc21   96-39858
                                              CIP

ISBN 0-385-48855-6
Copyright © 1992, 1995, 1996, 1997 by Robert
Bingham
All Rights Reserved
Printed in the United States of America
August 1997

10   9   8   7   6   5   4   3   2   1

First Edition

For Lucy

Contents

Pure
Slaughter
Value

I'm Talking About Another House

Max Drake and his fiancée walked out of the terminal doors and stood in a cab line. They were on their way to a wedding in the midst of the worst heat wave in Chicago's history. It was early August and all over the city people were being found dead in their beds. The local paper was a body count. As for Amanda, there didn't look to be a high probability of her becoming a statistic. She was a tall, big-boned creature with excellent circulation. She wore summer linens and stood in front of Max baring the shoulder of her bra strap. They were booked in at the Ritz.

Soft Amanda was sweating red wine. Max, who had mixed various medicines the previous night, was dying. He clung to the guardrail and kicked his bag as if it were a dog. This was not a wedding he knew a thing about. He had never met the bride. He had never met the groom. They were her people, her friends. As for their own nuptials? They hadn't set a date. But for *this* wedding Max had a plan. The plan involved a great kaleidoscope of social mayhem. The plan was to stay drunk for three days.

A lot of his friends were doing it. They were dying or getting married. A few were doing neither, but the margin was narrowing. Max did not want to die, but he viewed marriage as a kind of death. He was twenty-nine, Amanda thirty.

Amanda was "well off" in the cash department. She was a reporter for a respectably impoverished weekly. Her salary covered half their rent. Her dad took care of the rest. She had never paid an American Express bill in her life. That being said, she had been warned that membership had privileges that should perhaps not be leaned on in quite such an expensive fashion. Her Greek mother had given birth to a voluptuous raven-haired American girl with skin that suggested olive oil. She satisfied him deeply in bed. Max knew he would be a fool not to marry her.

They rode down the highway leading to the city in silence. Amanda had never been to Chicago. Max, who had some relatives living in the suburbs, had visited half a dozen times. He found the emerging skyline haunted with other women, with other times. It was a city they could never share equally.

The driver began to chat about the death toll. They were fortunate, he said. The worst was probably over. There was an interesting study under way in the paper. Blacks were getting hit the hardest. Ethnic groups with better lines of communication were suffering less. Elderly people needed someone to call besides a city ambulance. They needed family. They needed friends they could count on. Those with a network, those who could take preemptive action, were by and large being spared, those without were getting baked alive.

"What a nightmare," said Amanda.

"I'm glad your air-conditioner works," said Max.

Max had been ready for a ghost town. He had expected empty, steaming streets and a bunker mentality, but now at four o'clock in the afternoon the people of Chicago were out and about. Michigan Avenue was almost crowded. It was Friday. The wedding was to take place the next day in the cooler climes of southern Wisconsin.

"I'm telling you," said the driver. "You guys lucked out. Looks like you missed the worst of it."

"We'll see about that," said Amanda.

Two messages waited for her at the front desk. She was bridesmaid in the wedding, and reading the slips of paper in the elevator, she began to curse a Chicago company that charged outrageous sums for wedding apparel alterations.

"They take you hostage, these people," she said. "I hate this."

Max found women in the throws of neurotic wedding logistics reprimandably luscious. He gave his fiancée a kiss. It was heartily returned. He pressed his fiancée up against the elevator wall and stuck his tongue deep into her mouth. Then he shoved his hand up her linen blouse. The elevator dinged at their floor.

They mixed cocktails and made love. She was noisy and bountiful. Then she went into the bathroom to organize her cosmetics and toiletries. Max sipped his drink. Why, he thought, why would anyone want to throw this away? He made himself another drink and surveyed the movie list.

Now she was in the shower. He considered going for the telephone but backed off. He read five pages of a biography of Attaturk. Then he switched to a novel. Then he turned on the television.

"I've got to go out and do these wedding errands with Larissa," she said over her blow dryer. "It's a hemline altering thing, a strategy session."

"Fine," said Max, who was not a fan of Larissa's. "When are you going to be back?"

"I don't know, maybe an hour, maybe more. Are you going to be OK here by yourself?"

"I'll be fine."

"You're sweet to come to this, you know."

"Oh," said Max, raising his drink. "I wouldn't miss it for the world."

"I'll see you soon," she said, kissing him goodbye.

"I might give Carl Mecklan a call," said Max.

"Just let me know if you make any plans," she said and was out the door.

He went for the breast pocket of his blazer, got out the envelope, and dialed the number. On the other end he got her mother. He did not identify himself.

"I'm going out," said the mom. "If you have a message for her, leave it on the machine. She calls in for them."

Earlier that summer Max had held two short international telephone conversations with the mom. He'd taken her pro forma politeness as thinly veiled hostility toward his intentions and background. Now he felt certain she had recognized his voice, and he felt peevish and vaguely criminal for not having announced himself. As for the mom, he knew only of her complicated marital résumé and that she taught anthropology at Northwestern University. According to her only daughter, Mom had "seen the '68 convention coming" and had wisely sat it out at home. If he were to leave a message now, she might dial the number just to see where he was staying. Though the mom did not seem the type to loiter about waiting for her daughter's messages, Max did not pick up the phone. He waited. The mom filled him with paranoia. Above all, he did not want her to know he was staying at the Ritz. He paced. He drank. He was becoming drunk now. He flossed his teeth with his fiancée's wax. Ten minutes later he left his message and returned to the bed.

For a while he became engrossed in a movie he had seen twice before. When the phone rang, he wasn't sure how long he'd been asleep.

"Hi," she said.

"What time is it?"

"I don't know."

"Where are you?"

"I'm on the street," she said.

"Really," he said, reaching for his drink. "What street might that be?"

"Are you drunk?" she asked. "Because if you're drunk, I don't know if I want . . ."

"No, I was asleep. I want to see you."

"Fine," she said. "Where should we meet?"

"I don't know, someplace I can see from my window."

"What can you see from your window that catches your eye?"

"Gucci," said Max. "I can see Gucci from my window."

"What an expensive window you must have."

"It's a fine window."

"Gucci in twenty minutes," she said.

He sat at the foot of the bed Amanda was paying for, planted his feet firmly on the carpet, and ground his right palm into his left eye. Then he placed his fingers gently over his face, breathed out, and wept. He threw on his blazer, snatched two twenty-dollar bills from the desk, and bolted from the room.

In the lobby Amanda was fiddling with a baby blue dress wrapped in dry-cleaning plastic. Max, who had completely ignored the elevator ride, now felt as if he were falling. He took immediate evasive action and found himself in a small hotel kiosk that sold candy and cigarettes, scarves, postcards, and so forth. He took his time buying two packs of his lover's favorite brand of cigarettes and some Tic-Tacs and walked out of that hotel a compromised man.

He had time yet, and so he walked down Michigan Avenue until he ran into the hotel his great-uncle had built. Max crunched a Tic-Tac and walked into the lobby of the Drake Hotel. His grandfather had never gotten along with his only brother, the mastermind behind the Drake. Max's branch of the family had trouble with the Chicago branch. They rarely visited anymore. For Max, the Drake was a source of sentimental bitterness. In the bar he'd once had a disgusting fight about money with his father. Never mind, the hotel had been sold to a chain and none of the proceeds had spread laterally to his father, not that his father would have given Max a cent if it had. The bar was almost cold and quite dark. Red candles wrapped in a web of white plastic sat on each drink-laden table. Max sat down at a bar stool and watched the clock. He'd have one drink, one drink, in memory of his great-uncle and arrive at Gucci on time. If she were late, that would be fine. He'd use it against her.

She wasn't late. From the sidewalk he could see her inside the store putting all the other shoppers to shame. Max paused at the curb, breathed out, and counted to ten backward. She was too beautiful to be counted on. Her beauty scared him. It was the fucking gold standard. She was the most exquisitely charismatic lunatic Max had ever met. She was twenty-three. She rioted all over his blood. In early June Max had flown to Chicago to see a college friend play Ted Bundy in a play about serial killers. He had collided with this girl at the cast party. She lived in a loft with six other people. The sheets had been bloody. Max did not know if she represented his salvation or his death.

She let him kiss her on the cheek.

"You know, I've been thinking," she said. "I'm glad you never bought those pink shoes even in jest, because if you had, you might be a real asshole right now."

"Oh my God," said Max. "The chorus from the powder room."

"I've taken out a new policy," she said.

"Yeah, what is it? A derivative pegged to the floating premiums on my health insurance policy?"

He loved to confuse her. Though they'd discussed the topic, she still had no idea what a derivative was.

"You're so shattered," she said, falling into his arms.

A salesman coughed.

"What's the new policy?"

"Brutal honesty."

"Did you finish *Heart of the Matter?*" he asked.

"Oh my God, it was so sad," she said. "Reading that book in this heat. It was so sad."

"May I help you two with anything?" asked the salesman.

"Yes," she said. "Mr. Drake here would like to try on a pair of your pink suede or patent-leather shoes. He's been hot for them ever since June."

"Nine and a half, please," said Max.

"Vultures," she said. "So many vultures. Can you believe how many vultures were in that book."

"A lot. He outdid himself with the vultures."

"I've got to go to dance class in half an hour."

"Fuck," said Max. "Let's get out of here."

He followed her off Michigan Avenue and down various streets that hinted of inebriated familiarity. They ended up at a restaurant beneath a raised highway. The manager kissed her, and they were shown to a smoking table in the back. Max ordered a vodka tonic. She had a Perrier.

"You look terrible. I'm serious, Max. You better watch yourself."

"I've got to go to the bathroom," he said.

She was right. The summer which had opened with such ebullience, with such riotous glamour and ecstatic promise, had now faded into a bitter zone of romantic exhaustion. He splashed water on his face and took a piss. The feeling was that of great vitamin deficiency.

She was talking to the manager when he came back to the table. They were introduced. He was a square man in a box suit who appeared to have graduated from a bouncer university in the sky.

"So you're the guy she flew off with," said the manager, clearly disappointed.

"Yeah," said Max. "I guess I am."

"What brings you back to Chicago?"

"A wedding."

"A wedding, huh?" said the manager.

"Yeah," said Max.

"Well," said the manager. "You two take care."

"Sorry about that," she said. "He goes way back with my dad."

Then she flipped her hair back and adjusted her posture upward in preparation for dance class. With his elbows on the table, her beauty arched over his hung head in a disciplined, scolding superiority that frightened him.

"So," she said. "Who's getting married?"

"I don't know."

"I thought it might be you," she said. "I thought you two were going to tie that ribbon around some tree in Lake Forest. Then I thought, God, in this heat?"

"I don't know who is getting married to whom, OK," said Max. "Somebody said there's a Persian involved."

All that summer he had been the soul of disclosure. They'd spent a week in Rome together. The volatility had been tremendous. He had told her everything. They'd be sitting in a sunny park, she'd ask him a simple question, and he'd rattle on in an overblown attempt to captivate her with his humor and wealth of experience. The idea had been to make her kneel before the force of his personality. June had found him at the top of his game. Now with her sober and dancing in time to the routine of her city, he felt cowed and defeated by her charisma. It was time to play defense.

He asked her about a Chicago literary magazine. She spoke of the sorry state of the theater scene. When she stood up to go, he felt certain he would never see her again. He panicked. He tried to stand up but the room began to disintegrate, and he was seized by an impulse to do something brash, foolish, and not in the long-term interest of romance.

"I'm meeting Sally later tonight at the Drake," she said, peeling his hands off the back of her neck. "I've got to go. I suggest you get some rest."

"What time?" he asked.

"What?"

She was nearly out the door now.

"What time are you meeting Sally at the Drake?"

"I don't know. Ten . . . I think."

He watched her cross the street. A car came screeching to a halt in front of her. The driver was livid. He'd come within inches. The guy was about to get out of his car when the manager rushed outside and stared him down. Then she and the manager conversed on the sidewalk. Max wished she had been hit and finished his drink.

"You know what?" said the manager, suddenly looming over the table. "I've known that girl since she was this tall, and what I've got to say to you is this: You fuck her over and there's going to be the city of Chicago to answer to. The drinks were on the house. Get out."

The people were strong here, and as he aimlessly walked the streets shell-shocked and dazed, he sensed her kinship with the city. The mom, the restaurant manager, there was a suggestion of a network of blood conspiring against him.

He walked in square circles around downtown Chicago for nearly an hour.

"Well, look what the cat dragged in," said Larissa, coming out of the bathroom.

Larissa was a thin blonde who displayed what she liked to call "claw-back" resilience in the drama of middle-management magazine shuffles. Max found her sexy and contemptible. She thought him an emotional dilettante for not marrying her friend. Larissa and Amanda were veterans of the wedding scene. Last year they had traveled to Argentina together in order to see their college roommate "lassoed" by a wealthy rancher twice her age. They'd gone on the wagon for a month after that one.

Max counted the champagne bottles. Amanda was staring out the window, and he walked up to her and kissed the back of her neck.

"Have you made dinner plans?" she asked.

"No," said Max, relieved to have Larissa in the room. "What have you guys been up to?"

"We've been getting altered," said Amanda to the window.

"Carl Mecklan says hi," said Max, warming up to weave his story. "I met him at the Drake, and then we went around the city in his dysfunctional convertible, fighting about the usual things, playing music. You know, but I tell you that guy has talent. He's fucking going places. *Drag City* is thinking of going into publishing, and they just made him an offer . . ."

"Who is Carl Mecklan?" asked Larissa.

"He's a friend of mine who once played Ted Bundy and is now in the music industry. He doesn't fit your measurements."

"Max," said Amanda. "Carl Mecklan doesn't live in Chicago anymore. Last week he moved everything he owns to Pasadena. He's calling it a total love asset transplant."

"Maybe he drove back to visit his mother," offered Larissa.

Max poured himself a glass of champagne and almost vomited. Carbonation was not what he needed right now, and besides being caught in a lie, he sensed there was something else the girls weren't letting on to. Amanda moved from the window and sat down on the bed, fighting back tears with a tumbler of champagne.

"Do you ever want to build a house, Max?" she asked. *"Could* you ever build a house? If you had to, if the Nazis were coming, could you make a home?"

"I'm sorry, sweetie," he said.

She began to weep. Now it was Max who was at the window.

"Did you have fun at Gucci?" asked Larissa. "You know, I've got to say at first I was sort of torn. My feet were killing me, so I went into Gucci and sat down on a couch. Then I almost left because I saw you, but I didn't know if I wanted to compromise this morally handicapped tableau unfolding in the downtown outlet. But then I said to myself, 'You know what? It's just a pig dancing with a whore. Why should I presume he will even notice me?' So I got these really expensive new shoes. Do you like them, Max? Check them out. They're pink patent-leather loafers."

"They're nice," said Max.

Amanda was on the telephone.

"Yes, a residence in Pasadena, for a Carl Mecklan?" She spelled the last name out loud for everyone to hear. Then she left an unpublishable message on Carl's machine.

"Vagrancy," said Larissa. "Men are under the illusion its next to godliness."

"Thing about Carl," said Amanda, whose tears had now given over to the emotion of the corkscrew. "He always keeps his E-mail coming, no matter who he's sleeping with, no matter what town he's in again for the first time. Did you know that, Max? Carl and I actually exchanged E-mail messages at work yesterday. I never knew he was so chatty."

"He sounds cute," said Larissa.

He could have put a halt to this. The scenario flashed through his mind. That girl in Gucci? She was an old high school girlfriend. They were like brother and sister now, for Christ's sake, how dare Larissa . . . But he couldn't force the outrage required to sustain a lie. He couldn't summon false rage because rage was the only emotion that was keeping him awake through this maudlin self-pity he hated himself for.

And as for this sewing circle before him, he saw its poorly hidden social ambition creep like a vine up a cancerous spine. These maidens-in-waiting of ceremony studying the wedding pages as a horse handicapper hits the tip sheets, they'd get what their expectations had coming to them. A house. Max had never owned a house. He did not know what it meant.

This Is
How a Woman
Gets Hit

They cheated on each other. Now that was just the sad fact, but there was a difference in how it was done. While his flings lacked focus, she was singularly loyal to her affair. They'd been living together for three years and had grown skillful at dishing out abuse in a way that was quite memorable to both of them. On the morning this story breaks the telephone rang. She had a hang-up about the phone, and the hang-up was that she always had to pick it up before he did. From the bed he listened with his eyes closed. He knew her voices. It took about two years to learn them all. This was a what, where, and when conversation if he had ever heard one. Her lover was calling.

"Where are you having coffee?" he asked, sitting up in bed.

She was bent over at the waist with her head wrapped in a towel. When she stood up, her complexion was as red as the heart on the queen of all suits.

"Black it out, boy," she said. "Last night, black the thing right out so it'll never come back to you again."

Her southern accent, so often in remission, rose from the swamp of her youth to frighten him. She wore a pink nightgown and her dead grandmother's silk slippers.

"That must be the nice part about a real blackout," she continued. "The next day I can usually remember the salient points, but you . . . for you the humiliation is blank tape, isn't that about what it is?"

"Where are you having coffee?" he asked. "I need some coffee."

"You need a blood transfusion."

In the bathroom Ian Easley rummaged through her makeup bag for a Valium. Nothing. He dumped the contents onto the floor. A thin bottle of eyeliner shattered dully. He popped one of her birth control pills and got into the shower. Then he poked at his ribs. Some people, when they drank, got fat. He was getting skinny. He toweled himself off and shouted in the mirror, "If you loved me . . . If you loved me just the teeniest weeniest little bit, you'd tell me where you hid the Valium, Lidia."

She was dressed as if for an artist's funeral. Black tights, a mid-thigh flowery print skirt, black tank top, and shades on top of her head forming a headband.

"I wish Gida would stop making me have coffee with her in the West Village," she said. "It's like, 'I'm sorry, Gida, but why should I meet you at the corner of West Twelfth and Fourth Street? How in the world is that a corner?' "

By all accounts Gida was a terribly screwed-up girl. Her pets died awful deaths. People stole from her. From the icebox her roommates pilfered food she labeled under her name. Recently someone had ripped off her calling card number and dialed numbers all over Nigeria. Her health insurance policy didn't cover abortions because of a "preexisting condition." Increasingly, Ian felt Gida did not exist, but perhaps he was being paranoid.

"What's wrong with Gida now?" he asked.

"You don't want to know."

"Come on, Lidia, I'm sure you can come up with something eccentric enough to appear plausible."

He had never voiced his suspicion of Gida's fictional qualities, and now a serene glee stretched itself inside him as he watched Lidia retreat into the kitchen. Had it not been her lover on the phone earlier? Was that not the voice she used with him? From there deduction followed. Gida was a front, a fraud, a lie. A triumphant shudder of justification squirreled through his bloodstream, jolting his hangover. He took Lidia's keys off the bedside table and slid them underneath the couch. Then he began to dress. He put on his father's button-down shirt. He strapped on his grandfather's watch. Both men were dead, and in putting on their possessions, he felt quite certain that he would soon be joining them. He put on his jeans but couldn't find a belt.

"Where are my keys?" she said. "I have to go."

He began to tear apart the closet searching for a belt. Then he tried rethinking last night's disrobing process. Coiled beneath the covers at the foot of the bed he found his pants and yanked the belt loose. Then he stood facing her. The buckle banged on the floor.

"How about we go get a cup of coffee, Lidia."

"I wasn't a tenth as drunk as you were last night so I remember where I put my keys," she said. "I put my keys on the bedside table here. It's a habit of mine you should monkey off of some day."

"Let's go get some coffee, Lidia."

"No, let's play Mr. Logical Deduction. The game works like this. If my keys aren't on the table where I left them, and I know I didn't move them this morning, then Mr. Logic says this, he says, 'Who else in the apartment could be an agent of displacement?'"

"Maybe it was the ghost of Gida's cat," he said.

She glared at him in silence.

"I don't know where your keys are," he said. "But I have mine. Isn't that unusual? I've got my keys and you've lost yours."

"Shit," she said, looking at her watch. Then she began to scurry around the apartment.

She had a low center of gravity and wonderful breasts. As for her face? It was beautiful, but he'd exhausted her features. Still, it was not a fallen face despite the gray half-moons beneath her eyes. She liked to stab things in her bun of hair—snapped knitting needles, wooden letter openers. Today she had a yellow number-two pencil in her hair which meant she meant business. Ian watched the dirty pink eraser move around the apartment. When he had his sneakers on, he found her keys for her.

"They were right *here,*" he said, pointing down accusingly. "Right here under the couch pillow."

"You know what? You're turning me into a bitch, do you

know that? I have no choice with you. It's survival of the bitchiest. Do you want a Valium? You're right. You do need a Valium."

"Thank you," he said.

She opened a sugar bowl hidden behind the cereal boxes. "Blue or yellow?"

"Blue, please."

"There aren't many blues left."

"Blue, please."

"Here."

He swallowed it dry.

"Ian, why don't you go back to bed. Look, when I'm gone, you can go down and rent a porno movie and order out Indian. Isn't that what you like to do on a hangover?"

She had a point there. Why fight? Soon the Valium would begin to work on his rattled nerves, and then while he was waiting for his Chicken Vindaloo, he could dip down to the video store and rent something fairly hard-core to accompany *The Guns of Navarone*. He could get rid of it, switch tapes, and by the time his food had arrived, he'd be sunk in her bed soothed by the opening Technicolor credits of his favorite war movie. But that cushy scenario spelled defeat. He would take her drugs but not her recommendation, not today. Today it was the lie he was after, that was all he wanted from her, admission and confirmation of her deceit.

He followed her down the stairs and out onto the street. Her back, her nice ass, they hated him, but he had his keys and wasn't going to be drugged into submission. It was late September, but summer still loitered in the city. A hot wind blew westward from the river. She was a conniving cheat, and with the wind came a crusading zeal of inquisition. His blood was riding a great tide of righteousness the Valium couldn't hope to compete with.

Lidia stood on the street corner with her hand raised for a cab, certain that she had never disliked this young man more than at this very moment. With his pathetic mop of wet hair and unwelcome paranoia, he was nothing but a naked appetite digging its way deeper and deeper into her disfavor. For a moment she reached for the three men in her life. Ian was the disaster of her present. Her old boyfriend, the one on the phone earlier, he was the nostalgia of her past. Her current lover, the one sadly *not* on the phone, well, that one was easy. He was the thrill of the future. And what was so wrong with that? Was she supposed to cancel her past and discount her future in the face of this present?

"You know he's my friend too," Ian shouted into the wind. "I mean, I was friends with the guy before you two ever started fucking behind my back."

If only her lover *had* called, but he hadn't. Instead the coffee date was with her old boyfriend, visiting from another state. He was due to be married soon. In fact, Lidia had introduced him to his current fiancée. Marriage, it was an event, considering her life, that seemed sadly out of range. Still, her date with this old flame, it was harmless enough, depressively touching, nothing more. She wished she had told Ian the truth about whom she was meeting, but instead she'd lied out of reflex. And whose fault was it, if out of a habit that was just as much his doing as hers, she'd twitched away from his annoying little queries.

"Ian, I'm going alone, so please," she said. "Please go home. For me, now, just this once. Go home."

"But I've always wanted to meet Gida. If you two have some extra special feminine business to take care of, you know, menstrual cycles and boyfriend bitching, I can just shake her hand, have one shot of espresso, and leave."

"Please."

There were no cabs in sight and for a moment she was stung with a hatred for her neighborhood, its shabby poverty, its drugs, its lack of daytime taxis. She decided to walk to another avenue. He followed. It was incredible. He was either drunk and oblivious to her or so smothering with his rancorous attention that his company was unbearable. She turned to face him, to tell him off, but in turning, a cab's vacant light caught her eye and she leaped out into the street. A bicycle messenger swerved to miss her, skidded, and collapsed on the sidewalk. The cab stopped. The street froze.

"I wouldn't get in that cab if I were you," said Ian. "Not until you say, 'There's no Gida.' Say it and then you can go, say it. Say, 'There is no Gida.'"

As she reached to open the door, Ian spun her shoulder around. Now her back was pressed against the closed cab door. How many times had she flailed her fists at him in the physical feminine luxury of all-out abandon, scratching at his face and crying, and how many times had *he* hit the last wall of self-restraint, his fist raised and then checked by an unspoken code of behavior? He reached for it now, the last shade of pride, but found only a color and that color was red. So this is how a woman gets hit. It was effortless. With both fists he caught her beneath the armpits and tossed her in the air.

Lidia's head whiplashed against the roof of the cab. She collapsed onto the curb.

The bike messenger, his whistle still stuck in his mouth, threw a roundhouse swing that caught Ian in the ear, but he did not fall. He ran down the block. He took a left. He took a right. He found himself in a deeply Hispanic neighborhood and dipped into a bodega. There was beer, butane, and cut-rate cigarettes. A police car passed in the street but it was not for him. As if filtered through a seashell, the sounds of the maddening city roared through his ear. He paced. While pretending to shop, he pictured the basement of her building. It was nice and moist down there, filled with an industrial heat. On the janitor's utility sink he saw himself with a belt around his neck, but the image only sprung in him the beginnings of an erection. He bought a forty-ounce bottle of malt liquor beer.

Ian wandered the neighborhood. It would be cool, he decided, if someone tried to fuck with him, and he scanned the street for a young drug dealer to humiliate. He was ready for a fight. A dealer with peach fuzz riding a bicycle, it would be nice to break the kid's nose and steal his drugs. Ian walked down the middle of the sidewalk. People got out of his way. He walked and walked until he found himself in front of the video store. On a nearby tenement doorstep he rested. His beer was nearly empty, and he dug in his pocket and pulled out a badly mangled pack of cigarettes and a lighter he did not recognize. There was one cigarette left over from last night. He took this as a sign but what the sign meant he did not know. The cigarette was crooked, losing tobacco, thoroughly like himself, slightly moist. He lit it, took a long drag, and made a plan. There was vodka in the freezer, and now he knew where she kept the Valium. Already he was thrilled. All the ingredients for a recovery were there. He decided to make a party of it.

The
Target
Audience

La Guardia in the hot center of a New York City summer is something I'm secretly terrified of, and outside the terminal two helicopters crossed over the airport hotels. They went *cut, cut, cut, cut, cut.* I missed the four-thirty Delta shuttle by two minutes. Trump, Delta, the corporate obituary of the once reliable Eastern shuttle, the bankruptcies and timetable changeovers: all of it mangled my mind, and as I sat down in the Marine Terminal there was only one word for it: obscene.

The law is a service industry that never stops, and in this weather I've got to watch myself so that something terrible doesn't happen to me. I was wearing a light-blue suit with shoulder padding I despised, a white shirt, and a tasteful tie. I'm a pretty competent lawyer when I can concentrate, but it's no trade secret that I prefer doing my legal work in New York. "Let the client change in Pittsburgh" is my motto. Handhold them right into the conference room, where our climate control is superb.

The vaulted stone dome of the Marine Terminal marginally calmed me, but at the same time that malicious bastard I can be flowered in my heart. I wasn't going to give Trump the business at five. My meeting wasn't until the next day, so all this mental harassment the shuttle had provided was in fact immaterial.

I chased a Xanax down with a beer at the concession stand. It didn't take long, and it rarely does with me; my fleeting anxiety slid into a warm, municipal beneficence. The lemon-ish indoor light filtered down on the handful of waiting passengers, and the air was redolent of pending margin calls and the promise of a corporate restructuring. I'm in debt, too. My father picked up my college tuition, but in law school I was on my own. Bankruptcy law has its pathos, and when it passed my way during my first-year rotation at the firm, I came close to practicing it permanently.

Anyway, two and a half years out, and I'm still in the hole, and I'm not speaking of the wife and kid, because I have neither. I do own stock in a small-cap maternity-clothing line called Mothers Work, Inc., which has performed quite well over the years. Real estate is what hurt me. I took a mortgage out on a condominium near the West Side Highway at the wrong time, and then there are the maintenance payments, which make you wonder why you ever bought in the first place. Still, I live pretty well in the Caravelle. For instance, the building, with the help of the board—I became a member when they needed a notary—has organized its own shuttle-van service, which runs the long avenue blocks, eastward, to the 1 and 9 subway line. I'm a regular. The papers are folded on the plush seats, and another regular rider is a woman with Bear, Stearns whom I've developed a masturbatory attraction for. She's nice and plump, and, when I'm going through a dry spell, I have her down on her hands and knees in my mind. The problem is, we have one rule on the van—no talking. It's been two years now, and Miss Bear, Stearns and I haven't even made eye contact.

I read an article on closed-end mutual-fund performances in *Money* magazine and made a call to the secretary I share with two other associates. There were no messages. I read over a prospectus, but after a while I began to daydream and people-watch. The black company cars and yellow cabs pulled into that comfy little cul-de-sac near the swinging terminal door, offering up the five-thirty Delta-shuttle passengers—dazed yet earnest, purposefully relaxed, real pros. I sat there taking in the uneven stream of the white-collar world, the women in linens, the men a picture of distracted formality. And you never know when a seismic coincidence may hit your number: I thought there was something familiar in the way she shook her hair as she got out of the cab. Familiar, yes, the handbag—and, well, if it wasn't Vivian Tate, the girl I shot in the leg at boarding school.

What a makeover. The colorized copper hair, that amazing nose, the eyes that even from a distance seemed to have visibly narrowed since her youth. The killer body. (I could just picture that sculpted butt, forged, no doubt, in endless repetitions of that hind-leg kicking motion in aerobics class.) A few weeks back I had heard she was at Silverman, Bahr, and now it was as if that tidbit, offered one morning by a colleague well versed in the problems of my high school career—after I'd gone for years without hearing anything about Vivian—had jump-started the event unfolding before my eyes.

Historically, Silverman has never been a client of ours, but recently Bangs, Barlowe & Crumb dropped the ball on an important matter for them, and as a result, I'd heard, they'd been bringing some of their securities work to us. The news disturbed me, because the thought of representing Vivian in an initial public offering was frankly too much for me. As she began her migration across the rotunda—it was a perfect tracking shot from where I sat—I considered the statute of limitations on a crime that had been carried out at the height of my adolescence. I shot her in the leg with a pellet gun during my sixth-form year, and though I only meant to sting her, it happened that a piece of reinforcement metal had to be surgically clamped to her tibia. This shooting was not a matter I delved into when I passed the Bar, and there were never any official charges leveled against me.

Now she was only a few yards from my chair, and her sharpened profile had that latent air of feminine hostility, the look of a businesswoman on the rag and on the move. But there was something more there than the usual fendoffish-ness. She was on a mission, and she wasn't going to Boston, either. She was on a dirty errand to Washington and, come to think of it, so was I.

I was helping a group of offshoots from the Corcoran Gallery set up a 501 (C)(3) nonprofit corporation. The Corco-ran is something of a social client for the firm. In fact, I don't know why they use us at all, since there are plenty of Wash-ington offices to choose from, but apparently it has some-thing to do with J. Carter Brown, the Democratic Party, and a future seat on the Brookings Institution for a senior partner readying himself to be sent out to pasture. What do our practically pro-bono billing hours for the Corcoran have to do with the Brookings? I have no idea. That's all up there in partner land. The point is I'm beginning a new life, trying to get it together and not be such a criminal in the minds of others. In fact, the notion of me as an attorney is confusing to many of my old high school friends. In one department— the achievement-in-the-real-world department—I am a barometer of reform, and I like to see how it confuses my friends from the old days. They're not sure if it's the world that's changed or me.

I tailed Vivian into the ticket-sales area. She was wearing a pewter-colored skirt with a gold lining peeking out at the hem, which shimmied up and down her mid-thigh as she moved, a white blouse under a tailored black jacket, and pearls, gold earrings, and one of those bracelets as thick as a cobra with a rat in its stomach. When she stopped short at an automated ticketing machine, I joined her, and I'm embarrassed to say the chorus from a Hall and Oates song— "Whoa, here she comes" (it's called "Maneater")—raced through my mind as the two of us stood there operating our machines in nearly simultaneous computer palpitations, her gold American Express card inserted parallel to my green, our fingertips walking the walk, she a step ahead with the Delta Airlines screen shedding its electric-blue light on our faces. A late payment on my American Express bill came to mind, and for a moment I was stabbed by a sense of financial impotence; I was on the cliff's edge staring down at credit-card defeat. But the joyous clicking sound of credit approval followed, and the ticket spouted into my hand.

Vivian was at least six steps in front of me, headed for the security check. Apparently, I had no effect whatsoever on her peripheral vision, or perhaps her peripheral vision was not highly advanced, but more likely than not she had become a good blanket judge of character, and had sensed beside her just another burned-out attorney carrying that telltale brief-case around like a ball and chain. Women of her caliber have so much to keep at bay—and I'm thirty-one now and much fatter than I was in boarding school. My cheeks have ballooned out from booze, and my maid complains about excavating my shower drain because of the continual hair loss.

But I had forgotten what a sexy, clubby affair the shuttle is. I was always amused by the chic nonchalance of the men and women one-hipping their ticket-line stance, the mild players in the mutual-fund world, the lawyers like me, all of us half-expecting a celebrity-CEO spotting. We were ignoring one another as usual and migrating uphill toward the free newspapers and magazines—for we are, after all, the target audience. Approaching the security check, Vivian heaved that bale of hair over her shoulder in a kind of progress-achieved gesture that I appreciated. She had the trademark insolence— the bitchy, assumed equestrian grace—mixed in with the flashy hustle of Wall Street liquidity. But I didn't care. She was a corporate jewel, my victim, and as I tracked her every move a compounded sense of disoriented wonder filled my life.

Why had I shot Vivian Tate? The haughtiness we all put on back then? Well, the world has rubbed it off our faces by now, I hope. But Vivian was one of the shining turncoats—

that select group of control addicts who accepted positions on the Discipline committee to cash in on faculty insinuations that they would receive high recommendations for college. Members of this select group were known as "narcs," and would actually sit *with* the faculty, in the same *row* of desks, and vote you out of a high school career. Vivian was also a chapel-attendance bean counter, who paced the side aisles of the church, checking form lists like a reverent meter maid. Add that to her hand in the expulsion of two close friends of mine during our fifth-form year, and basically you could say the acrimony between us, by the spring of our final semester, had ratcheted itself up into a glorious boarding-school red zone. The problem was she was arguably the best-looking girl in the school.

I was two men behind her when she set off the metal detector. Vivian whisked off her clip-on earrings and her bracelet, backed up, and walked through again. The metal detector sounded, and, lightly stomping her foot, for this was not progress achieved, my victim said, "I have this tiny piece of metal in my leg. It's so maddening, because it's just enough to set these things off."

There was a pregnant silence: the impatience of the pack. A man behind me coughed and blew his nose, and I could hear newspapers being ruffled to jump pages in the background.

"Isn't there someone with one of those thingies, those . . ."

But a security guard with a handheld metal detector was already on the scene, and I fingered my penis in my pocket, standing the thing upright as I watched her lift her arms, hostage-like, for this shakedown—a form of suffering I could, in a sense, be held responsible for because of my actions so many years ago.

I can still feel the serrated plastic handle of that pump gun as I stuck it out the window of my second-story dormitory room. My friend Charley and a crazy exchange student from Venezuela and some others, the usual black-lung crowd, were loading up the six-shooter bong that rotated little hit-bowls—one, two, three, four, five, round and round we went in rapid THC fire, cranking "Love You Live" and hurling insults at one another. We were about to graduate, and I guess in the zeal of my loathing for the Harvard-bound Vivian Tate I pumped that gun up a few too many times. The sun magnified through the scope blessed the school's emerald lawns as I scanned them for a target, and when she came around a corner into my sights, it was a hateful marriage . . . *Puhhf.* She crumpled to the ground outside the fives court without a word.

Assault with a deadly weapon, assault with intent to injure. The headmaster was given two weeks to expel the perpetrator or the local police department would have no alternative but to conduct its own investigation. It was a witch-hunt of the first order, and since many of the younger faculty members were in fact dressed-up agents of the peace generation, it touched off a lot of soul-searching that was so sickening I just don't want to get into it now.

I didn't last long (and neither did Charley, who was later thrown out for lying in my behalf). One afternoon, I called my dad in tears. We loaded up the station wagon in the middle of the night, and I left that school forever. I did a post-grad year at an all-boys school in New Jersey that I'm still trying to forget, and now here I am, sitting next to my victim on the five-thirty Delta shuttle. We're drinking.

"I was just telling my ex about you on the phone the other night," she said. "He's still a caller, you know what I mean? I said to him, 'Carl, for Christ's sake, I thought you would understand what a restraining order entails.'"

In the half-pasteurized air of the boarding lounge, where the mouth of the plane came into view, I had tapped her shoulder. Outside, sheets of jet fuel reflected the comings and goings of the hybrid airport vehicles.

"Christ, it's you," she said. "Alex."

"Uh-huh."

I was watching the baggage riding up the loading ramp, and as she turned to face me, her familiar features triggered a fearful lust in my chest.

Now, snug near the back of the plane, she stole drinks. The first one was complimentary. Then she pilfered from the cart. That sent me; so wonderfully juvenile, the way she pulled those tiny airplane bottles from her oversized handbag on the way back from the bathroom.

"May I see it?" I said.

"Yes, you may," she replied, wearily hitching up her skirt as if she were displaying a tattoo.

"You actually left something in me, which is more than I can say for most men."

Outside the plane, the early evening sun was an orange disk above a bank of white clouds. Vivian's Bloody Mary was nice and sloppy. She didn't stir it, just let a pond of vodka float on blood, and when she hiked up her skirt for me, my view of her scar—a bumpy stretch of what looked like melted plastic—was partially cropped by the gold of her skirt lining.

"I was wondering about your statute of limitations in terms of any potential damages you might care to seek," I said.

"Uhhm," she said, nodding and leaving a stain of red on the brow of her lip. "I suppose I should sue you."

"May I touch it?"

"You may," she said.

Sitting there on the shuttle, getting tanked with my victim: now that's what I call burying the hatchet.

"So," I said, trying to muster a kind of casual ski-lift bonhomie. "What is Silverman, Bahr doing in Washington?"

"I could tell you, but I'd have to kill you," she sang back at me.

"Spare me, Vivian," I said. "What, are you shaking down Greenspan's boys for interest-rate information?"

The plane began its descent, and the conversation came to a loaded pause, with the two of us sitting there unbuckled, the empty middle seat suggesting a future, she with her pretty suede flats half kicked off, and a halo of bosses and stray clients she'd secretly slept with hanging above us in a stratosphere of money and intrigue. Her handbag was open on the seat between us, and I glimpsed the spine of Edith Wharton's collected ghost stories wedged between manila folders and God knows what else.

· · ·

"So what do you think of me now?" I asked.

We were waiting in the cab line at National Airport, which refused to move, squinting at each other through an awful Washington heat.

"I think the men at your firm are not half bad-looking, and they do their job. What I mean is, they're good at what they do, and I appreciate that. I assume, therefore, that you are good at what you do, and frankly I'm surprised, because you used to be so—I don't know . . . so greasy. But give a guy a few years, and you never know. The outcome is sometimes impossible to predict, sometimes inevitable. Are you listening to me?"

"Yes, Vivian."

"There's that, and the fact that you have a problem with women, and a problem with guns. You have a problem with women and guns and now, hello, all of a sudden you're a corporate lawyer."

Finally the cabs were coming.

"But that rat still runs your heart," she went on. "What do you think of me?"

"I have a policy," I said. We got into a black Alexandria cab.

"That must be new for you," she said, slamming the door. "I don't remember any policy."

"Here's the policy. I'm a lawyer, but I don't mix with narcs."

"That's too bad, you might learn something." Then, to the driver, she said, "1919 Connecticut. The Hilton." She turned back to me. "I don't associate with emotional delinquents in suits. How did you ever pass the—what do they call it? The moral-fitness section of the bar exam?"

"The review by the Committee on Character and Fitness? My friends lied for me."

Her meeting wasn't until the next morning. My meeting wasn't until the next morning. Our Alexandria cab took the long way, and together we gazed silently at the mostly vacant Virginia real estate that reflected a blue summer light.

"See this place—it's like Houston," she said. "Something like a thirty-five-percent occupancy rate. They went bananas a few years ago, then the crash, and now—what do you know? The lawyers get called in, and they're restructuring, refinancing, the works."

The air-conditioning in the cab was broken, and its beige plastic seats made my groin sweat. We turned on the driver. Why didn't he have a meter, and what the fuck was wrong with this city anyway, that you couldn't find a cab with a meter? We commiserated, showing our colors about the superiority of our city's taxis: even if they don't know where they are going, we told each other, at least they have meters. Vivian said it was all a District scam, and she told our driver where he could take his count. As we crossed Key Bridge and hit M Street traffic, our thighs touched. Then a little storm cloud of preoccupation passed over Vivian's face, and, watching her squint out the window, I suddenly felt the distracting presence of her deal in the making: "I could tell you, but I'd have to kill you." I stared out the window on my side and thought that if I was going to sleep with her I would have to get to the bottom of her Washington mess.

"Now you're supposed to reach up like you're yawning and put your arm across the back of the seat behind me," she said.

"I need a drink," I shot back.

She forced the driver off the road at a place called Dixie Liquors, and when she was out of the cab I went for the manila folders inside her bag. One was marked "SEC," and inside it was a deposition request with a yellow highlighted section that read, "This request should not be construed as an adverse reflection upon any person, entity or security or as an indication by the Commission that any violation of the law has necessarily occurred."

Second folder was a bust—just some IPO material; but the third, marked by a tiny yellow Post-it, was what I was after. It contained a handwritten letter on unmarked stationery, which read, "Vivian, here is a list of target companies for T.Z. They are: Tektar, Gamtrex, Colvan. As per our discussion Tuesday, avoid any overt quid pro quo for this takeover information. Instead impress upon T.Z. the fact that Silverman's contributions to candidates over this election cycle have no bearing on our municipal-bond dept. and *do not* merit the kind of negative *Journal* story we know he's working on. I don't have to remind you that publicity of this nature would—"

She was coming out of the liquor store. Luckily, a vicious sundown was in her eyes, and I was able to tuck the folders back into her bag. I was tying my shoes when she got into the cab.

. . .

A brass-handled, marbleized, nominally Southern hotel bar is an efficient place in which to drink vodka, and on our second double Vivian said, "You know, I'm sorry about your friends. Throwing them out, I mean. What were their names again?"

"You should be. They both ended up getting really well-rounded educations. Fritz did his thesis on the history of the boomerang."

"Well, that's not my fault, is it?"

"As far as I'm concerned, you have blood on your hands, Vivian, and it will come back round to you."

We both laughed.

"I'm sorry," she said. "It was a control thing. I got over it a few years ago. I think it had something to do with . . . something to do with food, but I'm over it now."

"Well," I said, raising my glass. "Welcome to the meal."

Men in tuxedos began filtering into the bar. They were slender; many wore rimless glasses; some had dates. Apparently they were all attendees of the White House Correspondents' Association annual dinner. I took a long drink and gazed at the cheap candlelit cherrywood heartiness bathing their faces, and it came to me: What better place to offer up names of targeted takeover companies in exchange for the squelching of one of those wicked *Wall Street Journal* hatchet jobs than here, at ground zero, in Washington? Well, what did they expect, with the salary the average reporter makes? This T.Z. was probably lucky to make forty grand before taxes, and then there was the world of high finance he had to move through. Still, it was pretty sickening, and for a moment I leaned back in my chair and considered blowing her off. After all, wasn't she the same bitch she'd been in high school, merely moving through the center of a different injustice?

"I've got fifteen minutes before I'm supposed to meet someone here," Vivian was saying. "Do you mind if we take a walk? You know, this is the hotel Reagan was shot outside of."

On our way out, she paid a porter ten dollars to lead us to the side utility exit that the Great Communicator had used on that fateful day. We stood at the foot of the building in the heat. It was getting dark. But as I moved to kiss her, Vivian turned her head and displayed her neck tendons, made a sniffing face, and, right before contact, crumpled to the sidewalk. The contents of her black bag spilled out on the pavement, and this time the sight of it all filled me with a drunken paternal love. As I leaned over to scoop up the cosmetics and paperwork, decorously holding my tie into my suit (a sure sign of drunkenness for me), Vivian reached for her leg in feigned pain.

"I'm shot. I've been shot," she cried.

"There's something here from the Securities and Exchange Commission," I said. "I suggest you start getting into compliance, Vivian. You can start by standing up."

"Oh, for God's sake, please don't read that," she said.

Down the street, a man with a red turban walked out of a basement souvlaki restaurant and stared at us.

"Get up, Vivian, for Christ's sake. You'd be nowhere without Reagan."

Then, from a police-car window, a cop said, "Lady, are

you staying at the hotel? Because if you are, if you're registered at the hotel, I strongly recommend you return to your room."

I flashed my key and seized Vivian by the armpits. "He shot me, you know," said Vivian to the cop. "The bastard shot me, and now we're going to be pressing some charges, aren't we, Alex? We're going to be pressing some charges."

"I see you two outside again in this shape, I'm slapping you both with a D.C. And that doesn't stand for the District of Columbia. Understand?"

The muffled sounds of great applause came from the adjoining room as we walked back into the bar. The President was in mid-address, and some tuxedoed attendees and, probably, opposition-party malcontents were having an openly defiant mid-dinner drink. They seemed quite dignified for journalists, but, then again, maybe they were congressmen or Hill staffers. Two out of five had the salt-and-pepper hair, and were no doubt drinking good bourbon—the Jason Robards thing—and three younger ones with wineglasses were laughing nervously, trying to please.

"I'm looking for the guy with the compromised face, but everyone seems to have this Three-Mile-Island grin," I said to Vivian. "Maybe he's in the other room with the President."

"Look," she said. "I'm going to have to ask you to skedaddle when he comes. Not that you look like a lawyer. I'm not saying that—that you look like a lawyer. Oh, my God, here he is, keep walking."

From behind a creased blue curtain mysteriously joined to the main dining room came T.Z. On his lapel was an oversized lamination, which he whisked off and gingerly placed in his pocket. His youthful, educated face and horn-rimmed glasses could not hide what I took to be the lurking financial disorder written in his features. I peeled away from Vivian's side and said to him in passing, "Missing the President's speech?"

"Excuse me?" I heard him say, and then came the double take and the tap on the shoulder. "No, no . . . excuse me, uh, how do you know Vivian?" His little worm face was right up against mine, seething with professional paranoia.

"I'm her broker," I said and marched into the lobby.

In the bathroom, I washed my face and drank some water, washed my face again, and pissed. Then I sat in the stall. It was a filthy world out there, and I went out to the souvlaki restaurant for a slice of pizza.

The doors to the main dining room were flung open, and I caught a frontal glimpse of the President beyond the metal detectors and drooping velvet ropes. He was perched at a raised table—flanked last-supper style by celebrity journalists, his glinting fork plunged into an invisible dessert. People were standing up now in the twilight of the dinner, schmoozing from table to table, some with their pigeon ears cocked sideways to their partners' feeding lips. Vivian was alone in the barroom, which I now saw was in fact the same room, separated by curtains and a rolling partition wall.

"I'm a whore," she said as I sat down.

"Really? I'm taking a survey."

The bar was disconcertingly bright, and though the red webbed candle holder in front of us shed very little light, we hunkered down to it as if we were in deep darkness.

"Are you in PR?" I asked.

"Damage control. Is that part of the survey?"

"Maybe."

"Alex, I thought we were operating on a need-to-know basis here."

"OK, fine, fine. But I didn't need to know you were a whore."

"This is the last time. I'm going to tell Bob I don't need this anymore, and I'm going to tell him tomorrow. He can just—"

"You're getting me off my survey question," I said. "And deviating from our need to know."

A gutter laugh from my victim.

"Does your date cover arbitrage?" I asked. "Does he write about the next company targeted for takeover?"

"He's doing a campaign-finance story on our bond department. We give a heap of money to elected road builders, I don't know. He's broke, but not as broke as I thought—not desperate broke."

"OK, OK. I'm taking a survey?"

"Shoot."

I was drowning in the pooled depths of a great flirtation. The vodka, the light, the pull of the declining ceremony next door, the partisan aura of the tuxedoed malcontents—for a moment the atmosphere swept away any objections I had to Vivian's task, and I was staring into the thing itself, the black hole of business in America.

"Here's the survey. They talk about 'tabling' summer associates at the firm. It's a sexual rite of passage that's beyond me. My feeling is, Go get a hotel room, for God's sake, you know? But there's one good one this year, and she's about to leave. What I'm asking you, Vivian, is would you lose all respect for me if I used undue leverage and tabled a summer associate?"

"You've never been tabled?" she shot back at me. "There was this one guy once. A big deal, very complicated." She waved her hand. "We tabled."

She *had* changed. Her crooked smile, her filthy errand—it had all turned a corner for her and become an essential hunger. The good-girl shame she had been suckled on had dissipated, and as we stood up I knew we had a deal. Together we went to look for a secret table at the Hilton, and it wasn't long before we found one.

Bad Stars

Listen to this. Mr. Killgore was hit by a trolley car while he was crossing a street in Budapest. He was a lawyer who forgot to look both ways, and the lead car humming along in electrical near silence nailed him. Nothing was broken but his head. He did not die, but he caught the whole thing in the head and once he got back to the States the doctors ... Well, they said he probably never knew what hit him. Now this whole event wouldn't concern me except I have never been a very faithful boyfriend to the man's daughter, Cynthia. We've been going out forever, don't even ask me how long, but for your own information it's somewhere between three and five years depending on how you count the breakups.

After her father's accident, she wanted to do it. How is it said? Go the distance. She wanted to get married. Bam. That simple. She said she caught a *glimmer*. I said, what? A glimmer of what? She said she didn't know, and as they say at the law firm where she works, I didn't pursue the matter. Brush with death, the fleetingness of it all, I guess it can speed up the mating process.

Before the accident, Killgore had a habit of hurling supper plates at his wife, Dumpling, and he enjoyed dressing down his daughters' dinner table guests.

"So what I'm hearing is you are one step forwarding, two step backing into a nothing career, is that what you are trying to communicate?"

Each morning Killgore was dressed by a Sikh attendant named Amir. In his gray flannels, white button-down shirt, and a homey navy blue cardigan sweater, he exuded the informal air of an impending weekend office visit, but actually he was an idiot who tended to stray like a dog.

The dawn of his legal dream had been blotted out by a millisecond of a miscalculation, and he was left to reenact an office pantomime of paper shuffling. Though he could not tie his own shoes, he still gave off a hint of his former legal earnestness, still managing the impression that someone was leaning on him for extremely expensive legal advice.

Killgore was a man of habit and the accident had the funny effect of reinforcing some rituals while discarding others. For instance, though he could not identify himself, he never left the apartment without sweeping his keys and spare change off his dresser. In the kitchen he'd stare at the *Times* sometimes upside down, sometimes right side up, sometimes upside down, like flipping a coin.

One day Killgore strayed into the Mount Sinai medical supply cabinet.

"Excuse me, sir, I'm not sure how you got in here, but that is the hospital's Haldol you're handling."

Mount Sinai had been a particularly embarrassing episode, and soon afterward, Dumpling had no choice but to hire Amir to see that it not happen again. Amir slept on the cot in the television room, and for relief I liked to smoke cigarettes and talk politics with him.

"Benazir Bhutto, she have the sex like the animal, and CIA they make movie. You know, porno?"

Amir added a lot, in a quiet kind of way, to the Killgores' apartment, which was squeezed for space by a no-man's-land of a living room. With its gilt-edged mirrors and straight back velvet chairs, the room was roped off in each family members' mind as if a murder had been committed there. To Dumpling the living room had once represented good fortune and the comminglence of tastes. The furniture, rugs, and prints were part Killgore's family and part hers, and when they had first set the room up in the early 1960s, it had seemed such a wonderful marriage, the way his father's bloody red (what Killgore had rakishly called "bordello" chairs) matched her mother's chaise, and so on. Now Dumpling stayed out for sentimental reasons, and Cynthia refused to enlighten it with the passing of her own social torch. So the dead room had a shrinking effect the apartment could not afford, and it left the family to slink around the box kitchen brushing up against one another in kinetic discomfort.

On this particular Sunday, it was Easter, I prepared myself to take Mr. Killgore out to the park. Cynthia sat bespectacled in her bed, immersed in weekend pro-bono work beneath a crinkled duvet cover. My little bird, the way she made nests for herself everywhere with her clutter of diet sodas and pillows, the clip-on reading lamps and pens, her loose thick black hair, and after work complaints that scraped at the litigious world. I loved her in that soft, vague way familiarity breeds. But after years, habit, once a friend, turned to foe, and a certain dread accumulated in the expectant labor of our bed. PTO. That stands for please turn over. It was the only way we had sex. There was that, and the demonstrative cruelty of our restaurant pattern that cursed our merry-go-round routine. But there in her bed nurturing the slanting Sunday light that seemed to draw up quiet shafts of dust from the carpet, she was mine. I was about to say, "I love you," when she cut in, "At least Dad got hit before he could find out what a shit you really are."

I pulled on my best Davis Cup sweater and wondered inside its woolly white world if I should put an end to it all. Just ask her to marry me and be done with it. We were like that, always on the verge of splitting up or making things final. As I've said, I have never been a very faithful boyfriend, but Sundays have always held a sexy redemptive quality for me. Naturally it depends on the day, but there are times when trading on forever can really turn me on. I mean the thought of those words—to have and to hold—the forever part. It's sort of thrilling.

Dumpling met me in the elevator foyer with the roseate glow of her after-church special, a mug of steaming decaf clutched in both hands. She looked at her husband and me with a stare of blind benefaction. This was a big step for Dumpling, letting me out on my first walk with Killgore. It was almost a religious rite of passage influenced, no doubt, by a post-coital discharge of a St. James communion. Watching us now in this touching scene of responsibility taken, she was letting me know I could be counted on. Oh Dumpling, I thought, Dumpling. The accident had sped up her marital expectations so that she probably imagined the tether of our trust rambling through the city's life as do those wonderful dog leashes that roll out from their handle like a tape measure.

But she was trading on margin with this account, or was she? To tell you the truth, with me, it can depend on the day. A friend of mine once blacked out his proposal to his wife. They woke up the next morning after a party, and he was still in his clothes, and she said, Oh, honey, I can't wait, and he said, For what? I talked to him about it. He said he wouldn't have proposed if he hadn't been so fucked up, but he said it's not a regret issue yet. So what if the announcement in the *Times* ran like an obituary. They're happily married now and not even thirty.

"There's a men's room down by the Boat Pond if he has to take a number one," said Dumpling.

"Is that right," I said.

I held the "door open" button to receive her last instructions. She was a fidgety woman, and since her husband's accident, a maelstrom of worries had incubated a layer of protective peach fuzz that carpeted her jowls not unlike the outgrowth from an anorexic condition. As for me, I have such blond hair it's otherwordly. A cherub-faced criminal is what I look like, but all in all I'm pretty happy. I've been around so many rich people all of my life, I suppose I've grown to look like one myself.

I pressed "L" and as the elevator began to fall, I goosed

Killgore's ass. A worry crease had aged its way across the man's forehead, running like an indented rivulet on a topographical map, and the descent of his black-rimmed glasses down his nose was only halted by the veined bulb at the tip. Since the accident, I noticed, Killgore had developed a nasty nose hair problem.

The lobby at 1165 was a mausoleum to outrageous maintenance payments. Usually it was a well-run building, but lately there'd been a doorman strike. Killgore and I walked out into the street unattended.

Easter Sunday had emptied out the Upper East Side to a stagnant grid, and overhead twister-tail clouds shot through the higher elevations while down on the street nothing moved at all. Even the usual placard-carrying doormen on strike could not be found following one another's tails like sleepwalkers in a circle. This Easter scabs watched over the buildings, money on their minds, sitting on their lonely lobby stools and gazing out on the day expressionless as hired mercenaries. Empty cabs flung themselves down Fifth Avenue, their lights lit with vacancies.

"I dreamed there was something rotting in my room," I said to Killgore. "I don't know what your daughter was dreaming beside me, but in *my* dream I'm running around trying to find the source of the smell."

"Bad stars," said Killgore.

Oh, the way I scratched at that family, ate their food, stole their booze, lifted their twenty-dollar bills, scratch, scratch, scratch.

The way I lived was twice a month I sent out invitations with a partner friend of mine. We invited brokers on Wall

Street and the derivative and hedge fund maniacs you can count on to drink, and we'd rotate the party to one of the five bars we had an arrangement with. It was like shooting fish in a barrel, my partner said. That takes guts, shooting fish in a barrel. I lived off door money, and a percentage of the bar. Weeknights I ate spinach and the lamb chops Dumpling broiled for her family. Cynthia was always up in arms about how her mother was "displacing" her food anxiety onto Killgore, stuffing him up with fat and protein for a heart attack. You know how women are, always querulously accusing one another of fattening or starving someone to death.

But Killgore and I, together out on the sunny street, we were above all that noise. I had gone to grade school in this neighborhood, and with my arm looped with Killgore's in a future-son-in-law slipknot, I was carried off by an extremely sentimental after-school feeling. It was of Mr. McClung's fifth-grade class leaning against the afternoon wind that barreled up Ninety-eighth Street. The breezy reach of that memory, with the screams and kung-fu kicking that chopped the air in such sunny alacrity, makes me want to cry now that this block will never change and that class has gone. We were fresh and jouncy then, marching ourselves in disorderly columns toward a future, less happy life, up the sidewalk in navy blue blazers, ties flying, and ready to kill.

Now with my attention span diminished, my mind dulled and addled by the premature indulgences of a foreshortened New York City childhood, I walked the street with the idiot father of a girlfriend I was tired of. It was a bad star. But I couldn't leave this family. Even the doormen at 1165 knew my name and registered their complicity with my intentions. Gracious and reptilian, they ushered me up to that apartment where the faint expectation of matrimony, quickened by the fervor of Killgore's accident, hung like the sweet and sour exhaust air shot from the delivery doors of Chinese restaurants.

Killgore and I walked arm in arm, and was there not a hint, a tinge of romance engendered between us as is so often the case with dependents and their walkers? Though I did not own the gum-soled shoes of a professional caretaker, there was the hatred each one of us holds buried in his heart, and the patchwork of gray hexagonal tiles that bordered the park, those well-trodden marks of continuum and fatigue, they lay before me like a carpet of dust. The empty city seemed witness to the day of my decision, and the incantation of Killgore's two uttered words passed through me like a psalm. Bad stars. Bad stars. They could not be helped. His only spoken words, they moved through my shiftless body cutting my blood with their poison.

Up ahead stood a lone hot dog vendor against the blue day, and I stopped to buy a Sabrett. I took a bite, and do you know what was inside? A string. I considered cramming it down Killgore's collar, but checked myself and walked on.

We entered the park at Seventy-second Street and found ourselves at the foot of a Pilgrim father. It was a perfectly still day, and patched through the budded branches of dogwoods were the sails of the Boat Pond. Killgore cranked his head up to the sky and placed his hands on a buckled shoe of the Pilgrim father. Then he wet his pants. The gray of his flannels moved to black, and a stream of yellow sprang out onto his loafers. Amir fed him multivitamins, and Killgore's urine was brilliant as the sun. He stooped and took a penny out of his loafer. Cynthia had put those in, the pennies, and though I could not see the head of Lincoln or his monument, in my mind's eye I saw the Great Emancipator pissed on, and yet the President sat there implacably indented in the coinage, still as the statue. "If he has to take a number one . . ." came back Dumpling's voice.

"It's old bladderless strikes again," I said. "What do you want me to do, get you a cup?"

All the old men with their tall ships were sailing the flat seas of the Boat Pond below. This slope was a popular winter sleighing spot, and seizing Killgore by the hand, I lurched forward and then hesitated. Once as a banana-seated bicycle child I had been taken in by an Evel Knievel frenzy. Joyriding my bike down this very hill, crazed in the green of my *Jets* jersey, I was ready for Snake River Canyon, but when I hit the lip of the pond, it sprung me so little of the air I demanded, it has forever let me down. Still, standing on top of the hill, it was a wonderful vision I had of Killgore and me flying down the grassy slope, whiplashing back and forth, back and forth, in the descending momentum of pleasure in death. Bad stars. Bad stars. The groaning man's incantations fluttered between the park benches, but could he stop at the pond's edge? Of course not. I flung the man facedown into the water. Turbulent little waves moved out from the epicenter of the fall, and the men with their tall ships complained their models might be broken, and the children hanging from the bronzed *Alice in Wonderland* figures glinting in the penny April sun were plucked up by their nannies, and the man selling Italian Ices next to the frozen duck shouted out blindly, "Ices. Ices here," and still the wind did not fill a single sail, and Killgore the sad-ass, his head struck against a rock two feet under, Killgore facing upward to his grave, dribbled his last lung bubbles upward before he got what was coming—a belly full of Boat Pond water.

But we are none of us the great murderers of our mind, just simple fools stumbling toward what is expected of us. We took a turn around the pond, and was that a smile of gratitude, of tranquil pleasure that lit Killgore's face? It must have been the day. It was a beautiful day. I would marry Cynthia after all. In the evenly spaced, reedy emerald green of the flower stalk rows, there appeared a plan. A thrilling feeling for Cynthia kicked alive in my heart. It was more than my Sunday retreat to the sanctum of her comfort. No, it was more than that. Her father was infirmed, and if I got married, perhaps we would be able to take this walk together again. Perhaps we would make these rounds for the rest of our lives. If the weather held to this pastel, if the sky gripped to its blue, it seemed a pattern to be repeated, that might never die. This walk around the pond with Killgore, it pleased me in my blood. The man needed taking care of, and there were worse jobs, weren't there? Amir could go, and I would move into the television room. The thought of a life lived on top of Dumpling in that home, it was a bad star beneath which I deserved to live. I would take care of Killgore and have children with his daughter. We would make more Killgores! The day itself said that. The blue sky overhead was a baby's heaven. I'd spill my seed on the race and get married, that's what I'd do. It was what was expected of me, and that, after all, was the only thing I had left.

The Other Family

When I worked on a newspaper in Charlotte a few years after college, I was assigned the crazy beat. Mostly I took stories from stringers and wrote obits, but they also gave me the crazies, so they could have fun at the expense of a new-comer. One day a man came to the entrance outraged, de-manding to talk to a reporter. He was a crazy, and I was told to go down and hear him out. Smelling sweetly of liquor, he had his story ready. It turned out that his wife had taken up with a police officer, and the officer had then stolen money from him. The crazy insisted there were ramifications con-cerning the police force, the court system, all of it. The whole town was involved. It was going to be a big story for me, the crazy said. My career as a young journalist was going to take off. When he asked me what I was going to do about his problem and I said I'd look into it, the crazy instinctively knew there was little chance that anyone would ever hear his story. So, to cut his losses, he hit me up for a dollar, which I gave him.

The reason I bring this up is that I was standing on the hot pavement and the glare was coming at me and the cars were passing, and I suddenly realized that this crazy must be some kind of relation to my dead cousin Drew. There they both were, forcing me to listen, making their half sense, tying *me* into their irreversible problems, asking it all of me, and the whole time preaching the way only the addicted can. If the crazy and my cousin Drew hadn't met in a previous life, they had passed each other in this one and were due to hook up in the next.

Drew died in Far Hills, New Jersey, a week after a check I had sent him cleared—and it wasn't just for a dollar, either. "A little sweetener for my head" is what he called it on the phone. When an uncle of mine died and left me some money, Drew said I had "won the lottery," and he saw no reason I shouldn't share the wealth. He used his frequent requests for cash to catch up "family to family," so to speak, since his mother and mine didn't have much to say to each other anymore. Their frigid sisterly rivalry had never really thawed, and this created something of a moratorium on inter-family communications. Drew wanted to change all that. He wanted to be the ambassador, to promote good will and keep the money coming.

It happened that my cousin's final foray into family diplomacy and his subsequent death coincided with my post-graduation period of sitting around the house. I hadn't done much of anything since school, and there was a lot of family talk about an upcoming "life choice." But at that stage I felt that if I were to make a "life choice" it would certainly set off a dismal chain of events. So I did nothing. When we heard about Drew, I was making a salami and cheese sandwich at our kitchen counter in Boston. My mother was eating a bowl of soup. She picked up the phone and began taking notes on a yellow Post-it pad. She said, "Uh-huh," and "Oh my Lord," and "I can't tell you how sorry." Then she hung up and told me Drew was dead, and that the funeral was the next day, in Far Hills.

First, there was the question of airfare. At the ticket counter my sister Barbara and I waited while our mother bitched about the price of tickets to Newark. It was outrageous, but the agent said we were lucky to get seats at all. The airline set aside two seats in case of family emergency, she said, but no discounted fares were available at the last minute. There was no getting around it, and why should there have been? Who could have planned a two-week or even ten-day advance notice that Drew would die? But my snack was good—a turkey sandwich with a package of mayonnaise that I smoothed out on the bun like toothpaste. During the flight, I took a look at my frequent-flier mileage. It turned out that this trip pushed me into the free-round-trip-ticket zone—and I hadn't even paid for it, my mother had. Drew's death earned me credit to fly anywhere in the United States except Alaska and Hawaii, so, if you think about it in terms of services rendered, the airline has done better for me than Drew ever did. Drew, as I said, always hit me up for money. What did I get back? Nothing. When I was thirteen he gave me one of his old sweaters, but it smelled so strongly of pot that my mother sat me down for a talk about zombies.

"You don't want to turn into a zombie, do you, Tom?"

My mother said that Drew was a fun guy but he never

"gave anything back." By that she didn't mean my money but things in general. She was right. Drew's contributions to community and country were negligible. The only institutions he supported were the rehabilitation center and the country club. Even in his last days, Drew was manic about golf. An overriding theme in Drew's life? Wood. With our grandmother, Nan, he lived on Woodmere Drive. He golfed at the Inglewood Country Club, attended the Woodberry Academy, and later was in and out of the Farwood Rehabilitation Center. The first time I ever got high? With Drew, in the woods.

They found Drew in bed. Like a car out of gas, he had rolled to a halt in Nan's downstairs recreation room. Hers was the last house in a migration from this apartment to that one, from one ex-girlfriend's basement to another one's attic. When there was no place left for him to go, Drew ended up back at his mother's, where, as you can imagine, tempers flared, and she refused to have him. So he washed up at Nan's. I remember her living room with its green-leaf ashtrays and floral prints—a real color wheel. And how strange it must have been to stumble in there at night or hung over the next morning; Drew's bong (the Purple Dragon) would bubble in the rec room, and then he would move upstairs to the love seat—roses and azaleas—and watch television. A tropical world, and Nan's pocketbook still a good hit for a fifty.

It was a closed coffin, and after the service we got into our rented Dodge Shadow and joined the procession to Aunt Simi's house. The cars moved in single file past the bulky trees and the substantial, almost manorial houses. It was a clear Saturday morning in Far Hills, a good day to work in the yard. I saw a man sitting on top of a lawnmower. He looked up and caught my eye. What did he see? I cannot tell. There was nothing particularly mournful about our cars. I was up in the front seat with my mother, and my cousin Jean was in the jump seat of the station wagon ahead of us. She had her back turned to her family, and this gave us a good view of each other. On one stretch of road the speed limit said twenty-five, but we were going over forty. The whole thing felt more like a car pool than a funeral procession.

I rolled down the window and let the autumn air in. The man on his mower, the big, knotty trees, the houses, the air—everything came around and revived us. I, for one, had not died yet, and I felt good and healthy driving down a safe street on a beautiful day in the shelter of suburban Far Hills.

"Do you really think he OD'd?" asked my sister.

"Yes, I think he did, Barb," I said.

"Quiet, you two," said my mother, as if silencing two children in the back of a car. And then, "Well, there's the Rutherfords' house."

One Thanksgiving weekend in Far Hills I went golfing with Drew. It was Friday, one of those unnaturally warm days in November when you walk outside and immediately feel cheated. Side by side, Drew and I cruised effortlessly up and down the course in the golf cart. Drew wore jeans and a tan windbreaker. He chain-smoked and bitched and rambled, shutting his mouth only for his ceremonious nick-and-waggle drive preparation. Also he was picky and superstitious about the color of his tees. Blue ones were for shots over water, red were for power, yellow for accuracy. When he looped the ball well onto the fairway, he said, "Sweet," or, "For my head." If he sliced it into the woods, he followed with "Fuck your mother!"

It was a good round, and afterward we parked the cart and walked past the clubhouse. There was Mr. McFadden, Drew's trustee, sitting by the window. He and Drew were involved in an ongoing feud over money. There was a second chunk of a family trust which Drew claimed should be coming to him, but the terms were tricky, and McFadden wasn't having any of it. He knew Drew was a sieve. When Mr. McFadden saw us through the window, he suddenly straightened up and gave a salute. We stood for a moment, dumbfounded at the sight of our own reflection obstructing our view of Mr. McFadden. Then do you know what Drew did? He clicked his heels together and gave the guy a "Heil Hitler."

"By the way," he said to me, the spikes of his shoes tramping the pro-shop patio. "I fucked his daughter last week. I fucked her hard, man. She was loving it."

At the water cooler inside the pro shop Drew filled a cone-shaped cup, drank it, and crumpled the thing into the garbage.

"Family planning," he said. "They've got to be kidding me—none of it until I'm married or thirty-two. That's six years, pushing a decade."

"What happened to that other trust you had?" I asked.

"Blew it, what do you think?"

Drew said he wanted to show me the club whole hog, so we were ushered into the Oak Room. There was this blown-up Remington print that covered almost an entire wall. It was a Western scene. A horse was being ridden by a man with a handlebar mustache. This man, in a double-breasted Union uniform, had on cream-colored gloves that folded back over his wrists like shirt cuffs. His mouth was wide open in a manly and warriorlike scream. With his long-barreled pistol pointed in the air and his highlighted red cheek, the Yankee looked a little drunk, or perhaps it was just the intoxication of battle. It was hard to tell. The horse was wild-eyed. A charge of some kind was clearly on. Beneath the print a ladies' luncheon was taking place, and one of the women didn't have shoes on. She was in her Peds.

Drew sat down and started talking about the terms of this trust he needed to get his hands on. First off, he wasn't the marrying type, and, second, he had been watching these shows on A&E, a three-part series on the environment.

"The ozone's blowing a huge hole that isn't getting any smaller, and in eight years all that ice flow ... Well, you know what's going to happen with that," he said. "This whole country's going to turn into wetland."

Drew couldn't wait for that: the golf course, Woodmere Drive, all of it—all of Far Hills submerged into swamp, and sooner rather than later if he didn't get his money.

I watched Mr. McFadden get up and walk between the tables over to where we were. He sat himself down right next to Drew.

"Gentlemen," he said.

"Mr. McFadden, how goes it?" said Drew.

"Fine, Drew, just fine."

Mr. McFadden reached his hand out toward me, holding

his tie in close to his chest so as not to let it touch the place settings.

"Hi, I'm Bob McFadden. I don't believe we've met."

"Oh, I'm sorry," said Drew. "This is my cousin Tom."

"I see," Mr. McFadden said. "Does Cousin Tom have a last name?"

"Yes, Nichols," said Drew.

"Well, it's nice to meet you, Tom Nichols," said Mr. Mc-Fadden.

"Nice to meet you," I said.

"I take it you boys had a good round of golf?"

"Excellent," said Drew. "How was yours?"

"I was at the office, Drew. It's Friday. I've been working."

"That's too bad," I said. "It's an awfully nice day."

"You're right," said McFadden. "But I enjoy it in here." He paused. "You know, Tom, as I get on down the road in this life, it's a little like going back to being a kid again," he said. "It's all about retreating to the simple pleasures."

Drew and I sat there waiting for him to continue thinking out loud, but he didn't. He just gazed off into this thought about returning to childhood.

"Drew, tell me something," he said, standing up. "How long is it that you will be living this way?"

"Excuse me?" said Drew.

But Mr. McFadden was already walking out of the Oak Room.

For lunch I had a hamburger and some cottage cheese, a Coke. Drew devoured a sundae with an extra order of melted chocolate. Then, with a miniature Inglewood C.C. pencil, he signed for the whole thing on his mother's account.

I stole that pencil, and after Drew died I taped it to a piece of string attached to a pad I used for telephone messages. It was a marker of our last lunch. But after a few months the pencil disappeared, and it wasn't until a year later that I found it again. I was down in New York, staying at a friend's house. We were getting ready to go to a party, and I borrowed his jacket. Smoothing down the outside pocket, I thought I felt a cigarette, but when I reached in to get it, it turned out to be that little green pencil.

"Hey," I said to my friend. "Where did you get this pencil?"

He said, "How should I know?"

It was a little before noon when we arrived at Aunt Simi's house for lunch. Everyone pulled into the driveway, and we all got out of our cars simultaneously. In their dark suits, my uncle Clarence and cousin Howard crunched the gravel looking like the Secret Service. In the living room, Aunt Simi headed for the liquor cabinet, which wasn't so much a cabinet as a closet. The double doors opened, and there were bottles of Beefeater, Canadian Club, Dewar's, you name it. Behind the bottles was a mirror. Even the ice bucket reflected things. Aunt Simi took down a glass. It was narrow at the bottom and wide at the top, but, unlike an airport glass, it held more than it appeared to, and engraved on it was a pheasant in flight. The ice cubes were the size of big dice, and they colored over nicely with Scotch. Aunt Simi poured her drink until there was a little brown pond at the top. It was her wake, after all—her son.

"Would anyone like a drink?" she said.

There was a general silence that resonated with protest.

I chimed in. "Yes, thank you," I said. "I'll have a drink."

"Good," said Aunt Simi, with her back turned. "What will you have, Tom?"

"Please, let me," I said, rising out of a deep couch.

"Don't be ridiculous. I'll mix you something," she said.

Beside her, I whispered, "Please don't worry about it," and reached for the gin in the back.

"Tom," said my mother.

"Mother," I said, catching an oblong reflection of the room in the ice bucket. It was sad, really. There we all were, my immediate clan putting in some time with the other family. It was ceremonies only, a wedding or a funeral, that got these two sides together. And at Christmas came the wrapped Neiman-Marcus reminder that there were indeed these other people, heard from but rarely seen, moving around somewhere in a different state.

A gin with some tonic and lime was what I made myself. "Anyone?" I said.

"I'll have a bourbon with ice," said Jean.

I hadn't seen Jean since she was twelve. Now she was nineteen and a pleasant four years my junior. I made her a whiskey-and-ice, some soda. Then, with my creased gray flannels hiked up, my belt secure around me, I walked through the middle of the room feeling watched and embarrassed. I handed Jean her drink and sat down on the end of the chaise longue where she was stretched out. I took a sip of mine and shuddered. Then I took another.

In this other family there was Clarence, Aunt Simi's second husband. His seniority in years had made him appear dignified when they were first married, but senility had arrived, and their union, once a humbling respite from both of their first marriages, now seemed shameful and disgusting. Clarence had suffered a minor stroke. He sat by the fire in a flannel suit, and there was something about his collar and the way the knot of his tie was off to one side that made it look as if someone had dressed him. The left side of his face dropped slightly. He was no blood uncle to me. There was my grandmother Nan, who was crying and patting her raw nose with a handkerchief. She and Barbara were very close, and my sister kept one arm around her shoulder and the other on her bandaged knee. The week before, Nan had taken her first fall. My cousin Howard sat in a straight-backed wooden chair. His boyhood mean streak had matured into an appetite for success in his career. Howard was a real go-getter in the software industry in Utah. Originally he had gone out West to explore a business opportunity, but along the way he underwent a spiritual conversion. He's a Mormon now. Holding up the caboose was Jean, who maintained a defiant generational split from the rest of her family. Drew, my favorite on this side, was not in the room.

"Well, he's visiting a better pasture," said Aunt Simi.

"A better pasture," said Howard. He was a bulky man in his thirties, with a receding hairline, and he had on square, buckled shoes that made him look like a sea captain. Everyone stared at him.

"Christ's sake. It's like a Hare Krishna," Clarence said.

"Simmer down, Clarence," said Aunt Simi.

I leaned back on the chaise longue and felt Jean's high heels against my hips. I pictured her tight cable-knit sweater and her breasts behind me. Then—incredible, really—the first tinges of an erection.

"Oh, Christ," Jean complained. "This is so pathetic."

"Jeanie," said Aunt Simi.

"Don't Jeanie me, Mom."

"That will be enough out of you," Clarence put in.

"I'm going home," said Nan, but nobody moved to help her up.

Jean went over to the bar, flaunting her familiarity with it. With a fresh bourbon, she turned to face her mother's beaming disapproval.

"Drew would have wanted it this way," she said.

Talk about conversation-stoppers. Jean slid in close to me, her ankles nestling softly against my hips now, looking for comfort. Three days had elapsed between her brother's death and the service, and Jean's mourning, once clearly tearful and heartfelt, had turned to pitched exasperation with her family. She shimmied down the chaise, and in my ear said softly, "If I can't get blotto at my own brother's wake, I don't know what."

I turned my head. "Got that straight."

"Not so bad for a first cousin," she said.

"Not bad yourself. What are you up to these days?"

"The usual," she said. "Want to get high?"

"Later."

"You name it," she said. "Later."

. . .

Later, Jean and I sat next to each other at lunch. We began playing footsie.

Since there wasn't much to talk about over soup, Clarence opened up with politics. "I just don't understand why you Democrats don't want to see the deployment of S.D.I.," he said.

This family—minus Jean, who couldn't care less—was what my grandmother on the other side of the family used to call unreconstructed Republicans.

"Well, Clarence," said my mother. "I think what a lot of people on both sides of the aisle are trying to say is that it may not be terribly smart to put such an awful lot of money into something that may not work at all."

"Lord knows that's sheer political demagoguery," said Howard. "And I don't think I'm exaggerating in saying that liberal politicians are on the fast track to becoming the Number One security threat to this country, not to mention a drag on good, solid economic growth."

I pressed down on Jean's toe.

"This of all times may not be the right time to talk politics over lunch," said Aunt Simi.

"Yeah, Howard," said Jean. "Why don't you skip it."

An awful partisan silence crept over the table.

The main course was Welsh rabbit with pieces of crustless toast cut in triangles. I mopped it up, drank my wine, and kept my head as low as possible.

Aunt Simi said, "You know, Tom, we hardly ever see you

at all, and Drew always spoke of you in such a kind and really loving way. What is going on in your life these days?"

It was too much for me. I didn't hate Aunt Simi for it; it was just too much. "I'm not trying to be rude, really I'm not," I said. "It's just I've been having to go to the bathroom for a while now, if you'll excuse me . . ." and I got up. It was true, too. I had to piss like a racehorse.

"What *is* going on in your life these days, Tom?" I asked myself out loud in the bathroom.

After lunch, Jean and I walked out behind the house. We were looped. The meal had turned lugubrious at the end, when Aunt Simi decided to make a toast. She had tried to be a good mother, she had done all she could. She was going to level with her family. Drew had his problems, there was no getting out from under that, but now he was in better pastures—and she stuttered and stumbled, weaving along in this vein until she was through.

The outside was like a cold glass of water, and we crossed the back lawn, Jean lurching ahead in her skirt and heels, carrying a bottle of Jack Daniel's. At one point her heels sank into the wet grass, and she fell down.

"These goddam shoes," she said. "They're just killing me, Tom."

We walked each other to the woods, and when we got there she handed me the bottle. I took it and opened my throat up to the warm give-and-take. Then she took out a joint and lit it. I gave her the bourbon and she took a slug. We looked at each other.

"I hate my mother," she said.

"Come on, she's not so bad," I said.

"Go to hell. You don't know what the hell you're talking about," Jean said.

I sat down on a hard floor of pine needles. Then my back was on the ground and I was looking up at the tops of the trees. Some of the leaves had turned, but most of them were still hanging on.

"You're my first cousin," Jean said.

"Yeah, my mother's sister's kid, that's what that makes you," I said.

"Yeah?" she said, and, hiking her skirt up, she swiveled over onto my thighs with the joint in her mouth. She sucked the thing down and then ashed it on me like a cigarette.

"You know, the last days," she said, exhaling. "The last days with Drew were all needles."

"I don't know if I want to hear it, Jean," I said.

"You probably wouldn't."

"What does that mean?"

"Your side wouldn't want to have anything to do with it, schlepping down here for a day visit. You guys didn't know Drew for shit."

"Let's not get into it," I said.

"You're a relative—like, I mean, relatively good-looking is all. But what I'm saying is you—you, Tom—you could be just another boy."

Jean's two eyes were a little out of sync. "I mean, the whole thing, you guys coming here, it isn't that far from a social call," she said.

She planted her hands on either side of my face and laughed. "I'm stoned."

She leaned over me and her hair dropped into my eyes,

making me squint. We kissed. After a few moments the feeling was over, and something else got in its way. She climbed off me.

"I kissed a married man once," she said.

"Yeah?" I said. "What was it like?"

"Nothing much," she said. "He had a mustache."

"A mustache?" I said.

"Yeah, he had a mustache."

"Listen, I'm going to get back to the house," I said.

"That's probably what you should do," she said. "I'm going for a walk in the woods now."

"Good. I'll see you, Jean."

"See you, Tom. I'm going to take a little walk. Say goodbye to your mom and sister for me."

"Sure," I said, but I was already turning away. It was getting dark, and from the edge of the woods I could see clearly into the house. Aunt Simi was moving around the kitchen, sticking her finger into the food platters on the counter. Upstairs, a bathroom light flicked on. It was Howard. He stood in front of the medicine-cabinet mirror with his hands in imaginary holsters. Then he drew and shot at himself. It was happening already. The house was falling back into something familiar and easy; everyone was settling down and proceeding as expected. In the hallway, my mother shrugged her coat on, and I could see my sister carrying my jacket through the dining room. We would be leaving soon. No one could see me, but goodbyes were already being said. I paused before crossing the lawn. What was I waiting for?

Plus One

For The Maggot

Then came the problem of the summer and the sense that we were about to become party to something disgusting. Roger and I were lounging by the pool looking like a couple of Hollywood schmucks with our fancy hangovers. She walked right through our garden and stood before us. It hurt. Her beauty had an air of corruption that screamed of youth and careless sex. She made our girlfriends look like saggy control addicts. She had these legs. Oh fuck, let's cancel the legs for right now, but there was another plus inside a T-shirt. Then there was the simple black skirt and her expensive-looking shades. I could see the bald head of Mr. Clean peering over the rim of her baby blue bucket. In her other hand she held a mop. Her T-shirt was a faded one and in black letters it read *The Replacements,* and below that was the word *"Stink."* I hadn't really listened to the Replacements since college. They had been a fine band, noted for their high level of intoxication, but recently I'd been worried about the legacy of alcohol abuse they'd inspired in friends of mine who still drank too much.

"You a fan?" asked Roger, pointing to her shirt. "I mean I'm surprised someone your age knows anything about the Replacements. Aren't the Stinson brothers old enough to be your father?"

"Why don't you talk about your father with someone else," she said. "Is this the house?"

"This is the house," I said. "Interview over. You got the job."

"Thanks," she said. "But I have to see the place first."

With my tan and comfy executive poolside lounge chair setup, she made me feel old and compromised. For you see, I am of the age that is composed of lazy summer weekends, of creeping out of my Sabbath bed after having mildly assuaged my hangover by slaughtering my girlfriend in bed. I do a few laps in the pool and for a Sunday communion wafer I take ten milligrams of Valium. Then I towel off and take up my position on the lawn where I'm ashamed to say I read *Barron's* with my Sunday *Times*. Sickening, and in a bathrobe too. Anyway, Roger and I were sitting silently in our chairs absorbing the fact that the maid had a sexiness that our girlfriends might have had five years ago if they had each been different women than they are now. It was a depressing fact at which to arrive. Now I'm not saying Roger and I thought the maid a better person or would even stack up as a superior long-term lover to the women with whom we were currently attached. She was simply hotter and sluttier, short term. She had a tummy that slightly canted her T-shirt out in our reclining direction. Around that smooth ankle was a copper bracelet of the high-end Brazilian tourist trinket variety, probably picked up while tripping on vine juice with Indians. Then there was a chunky silver ring on one of her thumbs. I've never really understood rings on inappropriate fingers. They've always slightly upset me, but this thumb ring bore with it such a great distance from the positioning of a wedding band that I couldn't help but feel intrigued.

But of course we had time against us. Our girlfriends were probably gossiping about who out of the house share was *really* invited to next weekend's barbecue at another house guarded by hedges and the handicapped. Recently they'd been sniffing around one another, the girls, trying to decide if theirs was going to be a relationship that might have a life outside the orbit of their boyfriends.

But the maid, oh the maid, it was like Roger and I couldn't even talk about it. Her white skin held no time for the beach. She walked plainly, slowly, with a perfect lack of any ass-shaking self-conscious style into our rented house. Roger and I were both recovering from the third of five weddings we were expected to attend that summer. Two more to go. The maid, in hindsight, had been sorely missed beneath those tents. She looked to be an attendee of a small, extremely expensive liberal arts college that breed the kind of women I used to enjoy conversing with about music and art before they took me home.

Roger and I looked at one another in stunned silence. Simultaneously we reached for the pack of Camels sitting between us.

"Look, I think I need this cigarette more than you do," whispered Roger.

"Really; why is that?"

"Because I like her more than you do, but you'll probably fuck her first."

"Give me a fag, Roger, and stop being such a romantic."

"She probably thinks we're off-duty narcs," said Roger.

"Speak for yourself."

Roger and I watched our girlfriends' mouths move as they interviewed the maid.

"Aren't you supposed to want to fuck the maid when you're forty?" I asked.

"Not when she's twenty-one."

"I bet she's more like twenty-three," I said.

"What the fuck would you know. Maybe she's nineteen?"

"Nineteen-year-olds are still baby-sitters, Roger. Aren't they? This girl buys booze . . . legally."

We both pretended to return to our respective sections of the paper, violently shaking our stories to the jump page in disgust. Then Carla, Roger's girlfriend, came outside with the dog.

"Honey," she said. "What Jitney do you want to take? I think we should get going soon before the traffic gets too bad."

Roger solemnly folded his paper and placed it on the yard.

"You know, I was thinking, sweetheart," he said. "I mean, fuck the traffic, let's go tomorrow morning, early."

I looked in the house. The maid was standing over the kitchen sink pondering our filthy dishes.

"But the weather's so gross," said Carla.

"I heard it was supposed to clear up," replied Roger.

"Where'd you hear that?" I asked.

"Umm . . . the radio," said Roger. "I heard it on the radio. That's right, it was on the radio when I went into town to get coffee."

"What do you think of our new maid?" I asked Carla.

"She seems sort of a nightmare. I mean, talk about attitude, but what are you going to do? I don't have time to interview maids right now. She says she can come late Sunday afternoon to do the dishes and clean, but she has some other job Sunday night, at some bar. So she's going to come back Monday afternoon to do the laundry. Apparently, we're practically neighbors. Eighty bucks a week, though, don't you think that's a little steep?"

"Hey," I said. "You got to pay to play."

"Exactly," said Roger.

It was shameless. Roger and Carla had just bought an apartment together. Then there was the dog. I got up from my lounge chair, walked into the house, and took up a silent position next to our maid. There was a liquor cabinet next to the sink and I fixed myself a drink. I rarely do this kind of thing on Sunday, but I wanted to see her up close and in action. She smelled of nothing. I poured myself a weak gin and tonic and walked over to the stereo to see if there was something I could put on that might impress her. I came up with a record of a band due to play live in New York the following week. The tickets had been sold out forever. The song I chose was a gem. For a moment she paused at the sink, smiled gently to herself, and went back to work. I was at once pleased and angered. I deeply wanted to talk about rock and roll with this young woman, and I wanted her to look up at me. It didn't have to be a big wide-eyed "I can't believe you put on that song" stare or anything, just a glance, an acknowledgment that I wasn't part of her problem; but I guess the force was against me that afternoon, for she did not look up. She stood there with her yellow rubber gloves sinking in and out of our little hole of weekend shame.

Roger and his girlfriend walked in, and picking up on the song I had chosen, Carla said, "Honey, are you going to get us plus one to the show, because if not, I'm going to go out with Laura Thursday night. In fact, I think I'm going to go out with Laura Thursday night no matter what."

"Good, then I won't have to scalp," I said. "That show sold out in two hours."

"I heard it was more like twenty minutes," chimed in the maid.

"I got it covered," said Roger. "Two phone calls."

The maid erupted into sarcastic laughter, a bad joke of her own creation, then turning to Carla, she said, "Uhh, excuse me, what's your name again?"

"Carla," said Carla.

"Well, Carla, this house is a little short on cleaning supplies. What do you want me to do?"

"Save your receipts," said Carla.

"I don't have the capital right now to create a receipt for your accountant."

"Here's a fifty," said Roger.

My girlfriend came up to me and asked if I wanted to take a bike ride. I said that would be fine. I like to watch my girlfriend on a bicycle. She has no idea what she's doing and she looks wonderful doing it. It was a nice ride and she wore a pretty dress that was perfect for the occasion and didn't get caught in the gears, and when we got to the beach, we went swimming and splashed like the lovers we are in the waves and biked home and made love again, and went back down to the lawn to read our novels. Now it's not like this house is glass, but there are a lot of windows and through one of them we could hear Roger and Carla fighting again, but it was not only their fight that was making it difficult for me to read (I'd heard the narrative before), it was the idea of the maid circulating in the upper reaches of the house that plunged my interest.

Upstairs, she was vacuuming our room. Perhaps I was being paranoid, but standing there in the doorway, I thought I sensed a touch of overzealous resentment in her vacuuming strokes. She had a Walkman on and I imagined she was playing some punkish number that was made to inspire hatred in the listener's boss. She'd seen our stuff, sniffed out our scene: a bunch of young adults who thought they were making it but not the way *she* was going to make it. We spilled a lot of sand. We left booze around. There was expensive luggage, and airplane tickets on counters. Looking at the maid work the wood floor of my rented bedroom, I realized she'd have no compunctions about stealing. But the weird thing was I didn't have a problem with it. My girlfriend was using the bathroom so I just stood in the doorway and watched the maid work, hoping I'd catch her stealing something so we'd have a secret to share. But of course she'd seen me in her periphery, and suddenly she came up to me with the vacuum on, her Walkman headset dangling from her neck.

"How long have you two been going out?" she asked.

"What year did you reach puberty?"

"Eighty-seven, Christmas night."

I fled the room.

At the office on Monday my secretary patched a call through from Carla. I'd been doodling on the arithmetic of the maid's age. It was a warped geometric pattern, perhaps a reflection on my indecision as to count back or forward from twelve or thirteen.

"Did you leave money for the gardener?" she asked.

The gardener wasn't exactly a gardener. The gardener was a team of Hispanic lawn-care people who came and mowed the lawn and clipped things. It was an expense I hadn't counted on when I went in on the house share.

"Yes, Carla," I said. "As you pointed out, it was my week for lawn care. I took care of it. Forty dollars, in the bowl."

"Really?"

"Of course. What happened?"

"The guy called me at work. Can you believe that? He said the bowl was empty."

"Didn't Sam say he was going to come out on Monday to write?" I asked.

"I already called him," replied Carla. "He's feigning ignorance, but I bet it was the maid. I don't know. I found her sort of passive-aggressive, didn't you?"

"Oh, Jesus Christ, Carla," I replied.

"I'm worried about my earrings," she said. "I left my favorite earrings on the bedside table. I bet she'll be wearing them in whatever fashion hole she likes to crawl into during the week."

"Carla," I said. "The lawn-care people annoy you at work and now I'm hearing about earrings at work. Why don't we both go back to work?"

"Ohh," said Carla. "Well, I'm sorry to take up your precious time. I just thought you'd like to know you're getting ripped off."

I adore Sam, but he has this nasty habit of getting up to go to the bathroom in the late innings of a restaurant party and never returning to pay for his veal. Sam had opted for half payment on his slice of the share. He rarely came out on weekends. He'd usually go against the traffic on Sunday nights and sleep in the master bedroom all week. Clearly he was fucking the maid. Sam is a writer and you know how those guys are—always slinking and sidling over back garden gates with that off-timing charisma. Suddenly I was furious. Sam hated Carla's guts, but probably didn't know that it was my money he and the maid were drinking up. There had been some backstabbing lawn-care financing confusion in this house share, couples scraping for a moral high ground on the subject of the divisor when it came to food and lawn-care expense. Some, like me, had opted for no lawn care at all. But lawn care was not what was bothering me now. It was the image of Sam and the maid splitting the forty dollars I'd left in the bowl and going out for drinks together.

"I don't know what to tell you, Carla," I said. "There's nothing we can do but see if a pattern develops."

"You're sure you put your money in?"

"Positive."

"Well, goddam it!" she said and hung up.

On Thursday night Roger and I arrived to see the sold out concert in a black company sedan. Getting out of that car, I got to say, I picked up a bit of hostility emanating from the youth loitering outside. It wasn't as if we were two scabs crossing a picket line, it was more like a little splash of urban disdain was spat our way. Roger, God bless him, is the greatest snob of rock snobs and as a rule prefers to go to shows where his weight and influence as a journalist can get him on some list. Sometimes I follow.

"Clueless jam kids," snarled Roger. "Looking for a leader."

There was a small line for the rock elite waiting at a side box-office window. The women were better dressed here. Someone touched me on the shoulder. I turned around. It was the maid.

"Hey," I said.

It was difficult to know what to do. A kiss was certainly not in order but then again neither was a handshake. We stood there on the street not touching. Roger was at the window.

"Wouldn't you know. Of all people, you guys would get in free," she said.

"Whoever said rock was fair," I said.

"Not me."

"From the looks of it, you must be on the list too," I said.

"I deserve to be."

"Is that right."

"Yeah, I'm plus one. I went out with Mark Sandburn for nearly a year."

"Yeah, what happened? He set fire to your cat?"

I stood there in the street stunned. Mark Sandburn was something of a minor hero of mine. She was wearing a silver top that was all about refracting light and foregrounding breasts, and her pants had a wonderful relationship to her hips. Then there were her jewelry and earrings. She was her own fucking light show.

"That idiot Blumstein," said Roger, turning to me. "I told him get me a plus one but . . ."

"But they only comped you," said the maid. "I didn't know this was going to be an industry show."

"You," said Roger. "What are *you* doing here?"

"She's here to play a golden oldie with Mark Sandburn," I said.

"You know you guys shouldn't be so mean," said the maid. "Mark made sure I'm plus one, but my girlfriend decided to have dinner with some guy who just threw himself into the East River."

Roger and I stood aside as she did her thing at the window.

"Here," she said, presenting me with a ticket. "Chalk it up to a miracle."

We walked into the show together, like a date. Someone with a clipboard and a headset gave us each a fluorescent wrist band and a rectangular patch to place on our person. So there we were, the maid and I standing around with all the little badges of honor that allow one to drink at the bar where others can't drink, and march through those wide-bodied bouncers, those sentinels of the stuffed velvet ropes, so as to reach the little secret places others are blocked from and go backstage and be almost as cool as the cool stars. The fucking hierarchies of rock, it was medieval.

"I won't charge you for the ticket," she said. "But you have to buy me drinks all night because I expect to be treated like a queen when I'm at a show, especially this one. Like you can start by lighting my cigarette. What's your name anyway? Mind if I call you 'Rocko'? This show has been sold out for weeks, so I get to call you Rocko, OK. So, Rocko, why don't you get me a Sea Breeze? Don't fuck it up. You got a house in the fucking Hamptons with chicks who probably leave their IQ in Prada bags by the pool, and if I say I want a drink, I expect you to hop to it. Are you listening?"

I was glad to see the maid transformed, but I did not get her a drink. She already had one. I watched various people, mostly male, engage the maid in conversations that came to me as splintered shards of tonal disdain. This was all going on above one of the opening bands I'd never heard of. Then Roger came up and suggested we light this guy Tim Nye's red hair on fire. I dug out my Zippo.

"Let's scrotch that Alterna-Trump. I mean, fuck, let's hunt him down."

But before I could leave, the maid said, "Rocko, get busy on that Sea Breeze."

I returned with the drinks after being purposely ignored by the VIP bartender because I didn't arrive at his preconceived notion of what was an important rock groupie or critic.

There was a change onstage, and then a band I'd heard of vaguely was playing music I couldn't understand. We were on a balcony behind the ropes and the band served as evil cock-tail mixer music that shortened people's sentences to insults.

Roger was going on about the finances of a Tim Nye record label deal.

"Yeah, I heard the Maggot securitized the loan with some option on his grandmother's future death. Can you believe that? I was thinking the other day, someone should create a derivative based on the Maggot's . . ."

"So how long has your girlfriend been on the pill?" the maid cut in.

"I don't know."

"I mean, did she get it going with the pill when you two started fucking?"

"My girlfriend has a history of promiscuity I happen to cherish."

"Really," said the maid, shaking her hair out of a bun.

"Really."

"Who was she fucking before she got around to you?"

The band was launching into something loud, each young man believing his guitar to be the ax of his uncompromising chopping capabilities.

Finally the band the house had come to see, know, and love arrived and the maid and I together went downstairs and rammed ourselves up front, for we both sensed in one an-other the aficionado, and after that, it doesn't matter any-more. All the structural problems of money, age, and achieve-ment collapsed like pickup pixie sticks spilled onto the floor of childhood and we were cast off spinning, listening to the music we loved betwixt an elliptical rubber band of sexual tension, and the occasional touching of arms. Between sets I got her more drinks. I even fooled her into thinking I wasn't another symbol of the capitalistic patriarchy that I actually am, which was fun. But of course she wouldn't go home with me. Clearly, she said, I was perverted and washed up. She had a boyfriend six years my junior that "gave her what she needed."

But we did play a straight set after the show. She gave me that at least, the maid, a summer walk in the city. And we didn't go to a coffee shop either. We had a drink at a pleasant bar and talked about music, jobs, and literature, and she even asked the cocktail waitress for a pen. I'd convinced her I wasn't part of her problem and for me that was enough. Then we left and walked the right angles of our city, commenting on the weather, until we arrived at a wall. She let herself be turned round so gracefully, expectantly, and up against that wall with the nearly vacant summer city a lonely witness, we parted with bits of blissful lip service.

Doubles

She had a crisp forehand and a late seventies two-handed backhand reminiscent of Tracy Austin. The court was clay, and skidding into his opening shots, Alex tried not to seize up, but the prospect of being joined by tennis-ball-batting children was too much for him. His first balls flew long. She, on the other hand, was a most professional recreator from the first shot.

"Bet you didn't know I had a child," she said.

"What?" he replied, punching a forehand cross-court into the net.

"A child," she said. "From my first marriage."

"When did you have it?"

"You don't want to know, and frankly I reserve the right not to tell you."

"I'm sorry I can't hear you in this wind. Did it hurt?"

"What?"

"Having a child. Did it hurt?"

"It is a pain you'll never know."

As they hit, his initial peril dropped off into the first feeling of skidded clay court timing.

"Here come the kids," she said.

Earlier that day Alex's mother had received the news that a close friend of her dead husband had expired himself. Alex, who was on vacation, did not want to go to a funeral, and so on a clear blue morning in August he found himself driving his mother to the airport. The funeral was in Boston. Outside the airport his mother kept up the pleading, humiliating herself as usual. It was incredible the persistence of that woman. All the way in the car she'd said things like . . . "After everything Mr. Rittenhouse did for your father . . ." and . . . "How much was your starting salary at that job he got you . . ." and . . . "You're actually repaying a freshly dead man by going off to play tennis!"

"I'm sorry, Mother," said Alex.

"If I could make you, I'd make you," she said. "But I can't. I can't make you do *any*thing anymore."

It was a light travel day in the middle of the week. Idle cab drivers loitered against the terminal wall.

"Why won't you come?"

Alex helped his mother with her bags, gave her a kiss, got back in the car, and closed the door. From the curb she shot him that forlorn look of abandonment, the look of age. It was cruel being a son. He felt its cruelty, its defiant selfishness. His mother had always played to his emotionally lazy side and because theirs was a family of two, this was not the first time there had been a kind of lover's quarrel over travel plans. He started the engine and waved her into a reverse, receding loneliness. There she was, a widow performing a widow's duty, crestfallen and grieving not for Mr. Ritten-house, but for the cold monotony of lonely old age his death reaffirmed.

On the road to town he became sickened by the age of his tennis date. She was much younger than his mother, but they *did* know one another. They were friends, or as good acquaintances as any two women on opposite ends of middle age could be. They had in common an interest in the Democratic Party and got together a half-dozen times a year to have their checking accounts raided in return for that proud feeling of having had a hand in the process.

Alex did not call his approaching tennis date Anne, and he did not call her Mrs. Phillips. He called her nothing at all. What *was* clear was that Anne Phillips had married an enormously wealthy man many years her senior, and, yes, it was rumored to be an unhappy arrangement.

Money, age, and marriage, they were a perplexing mystery of timing he felt fated to fuck up. Probably he would get married too late to some self-serving young sex kitten, or else too early to a menopausal heiress, or not get married at all, or . . . Well, screw it. It did not matter. Today was day five of his vacation from the currency trading desk, and released from the prospect of a Boston funeral, he had nothing to complain about. Nothing to complain about at all.

He called the spread in age of the various women he was attracted to "range." An example of range? The weeping University of Vermont hitchhiker he'd had in the car the other night. How sad was that? She'd spewed a tale of drunken boyfriend betrayal and all of it set at a bar she called The Box. She'd literally cried on his shoulder. He'd considered doing something degrading to her back at the house, but he hadn't had enough energy to take advantage of her grief. Then there were women his own age like Vivian Tate. Now Vivian was right smack in the middle of his range, but after their disastrous vacation together in the Bahamas, she'd opted for a "significant cooling-off period." A cold E-mailist was that Vivian, and she hadn't approved of him switching from the law to currency trading one bit. That left Anne Phillips, who was certainly pushing the older reaches of range, but she wasn't the only preservation junkie at the club. There was a bevy of them, and during the week they were *so* underutilized, what with their husbands working on the mainland and their kids off at some expensively supervised sailing activity.

He passed Cumberland Farms and hit the traffic leading into town. There was no escaping the summer sprawl, daytrippers shopping in T-shirt stores, muscular college kids with fluorescent colored sunblock on their noses flip-flopping about the streets or driving cars that were a confetti of alma mater bumper stickers. He was relieved when he finally pulled into the yacht club's parking lot. Why was it he felt as if he were having an affair already? Perhaps it was the way she had suggested doubles to blunt the discrepancy in their age?

"Doubles would be fun, don't you think?" she had insisted. "Don't you think."

In the corridors between courts, the green fence covers fluttered and clanked in the wind. She was hiding from the sun beneath an umbrella strapping on a tennis elbow brace. She had flat, brittle blond hair and a face of neutral beauty that held a latent sense of cold cream and moisturizing lotion application. Epidermal aging, it was a battle, and the enemy had been held at bay long enough for her to linger in a vacuum of indeterminate age. She wasn't at all tan, but looking into the milky spangles of her blue irises, it seemed to Alex as if he had arrived at the gateway to leisure.

"Now," she said, looking at him quizzically. "Are we going to be a good boy?"

It was his line from her party the previous night. He had been seated on her left, but instead of making lively political banter, he had fallen silent before his moody self-perception as a drone, a working stiff, a conservative young man too old for the college crowd, but distinctly separate too from the Democratic Party intelligentsia that gathered each summer at the Phillipses' table. It was just about enough to make him change party affiliation, this altruism, this talk of the country as a focus group of voting habits spreading westward from these bluefish dinners. He felt tired, charmless, and in the midst of a tax revolt. "Terrible job I have, and two days out of every five I work for the government." Were those not Mr. Rittenhouse's last words to him last summer? But no one at the table seemed to care. Breezy with wealth, they expected of him a pointed economic perspective on their foreign policy debates and political horse races. But he had nothing to offer. He had not recently returned from a war-torn Asian country as had the incredibly drunk, jet-lagged journalist across the table. He was not a liberal syndicated columnist nor a political media consultant running five ad campaigns at once, nor was he the second wife of a political fund-raiser angling hard for the ambassadorship to Mauritius. He was not a member of the Council on Foreign Relations, or a Middlebury lacrosse jock. He felt he had little in common with the corporate antagonism coming from the environmental consultant across the way. He was a thirty-two-year-old currency trader on vacation with his mother, and he was miserable.

"So," she had said over dessert. "What do you want to be in your life?"

He hated it when grown-ups opened with the big question, but his discomfort was so intertwined with these plentifully stretched adult breasts cresting and falling in his downward glance that he answered, "A good boy."

The kids arrived in defiance of the all whites rule of the club. Day-Glo stripes and garish patterns splashed across their midsections. The boy bounced the strings of his oversized racket on his downy head. They were a barely pubescent couple, strangely hatched with the boy shooting sideways glances of suspicion and apathy. At least the girl seemed eager to play. Her name was Melissa, and she sang back her mother's greeting in a tennis dress cleaved with innumerable white pleats.

"Melissa, this is Mr. Spring. He's a . . . well, what exactly are you, Mr. Spring?"

"I'm a childless trader living in New York."

"He's a lonely young man who's here to see if Mummy got her money's worth at camp. Now, how should we do this, Alex? I'm not sure if I should entrust you with my daughter, but I suppose I have no choice."

"Trade what?" asked Fritz.

"Money," said Alex.

That shut everyone up, and it segued nicely into a down the line doubles warm-up. The kids could hit. They had met at tennis camp. She was fourteen and a *half*, she insisted. He was fifteen. But as the first balls flew, Alex found himself thrown off-kilter by the brazen coupleness of these two. What did they do with one another off the court? He didn't want to think about it. A tennis camp romance was one thing, but the notion of the two of them carrying on an unsupervised fumbling of one another's budding little bodies in that overdecorated house on Totem Point . . . He tried to put it out of his mind, but Fritz had already spotted his weak backhand. Terrifying. They had probably taught him that at camp, identify the opponent's weakness early. But what was worse was Alex couldn't help hitting mistaken cross-court shots that landed right at Mother's feet. One even ricocheted onto the neighboring court.

Tennis anxiety among strangers. It was an especially acute pain, and for a moment he wished he were buckled in beside his mother on the plane. Filial obligation required no coordination, only rote gestures, and was there not refuge to be taken in funereal platitudes? But instead of comforting his mother, instead of honoring the memory of his dead father's friend, he was facing the tepid seduction of a woman suffering from tennis elbow in full view of children.

"Up or down," said Anne Phillips, spinning her racket on the court.

"Down," said Melissa.

It was down, and he did not feel like serving. The thought

of serving to Fritz with those ridiculous sneakers sparkling reflector lights at every step, it was too much for him. But Melissa tossed him the brand-new balls anyway.

"I'll need a few practice," he said.

And it was a disaster. Two balls hopelessly long, another in the net, and everyone standing there on a miswired court twirling their rackets at him in disdain. The toss raised his eyes directly into the sun, blinding him. He began seeing spots and various streaks of annoying color. His whole life seemed a stupendous failure. His job was a zero-sum-end game of yen put warrants and international interest rate graphs, and it wasn't as if he helped *make* anything either. Sickening. His claustrophobic apartment in that awful high-rise near the West Side Highway with its heavy maintenance payments, his happy hour financial friendships with married commuters, sad blind dates, and credit card debt, they all stacked up against him as he thundered two more worthless practice serves long.

At the service line he hung his head and bounced the ball as if waiting for his own beheading. He wished not for death but to be absent from his life. He would have to breathe. He turned to face the back fence and methodically hopped stray balls into his pockets.

"These are good," he croaked.

By the grace of God his first serve was in, and incredibly he and Melissa won the point. He served the game out, and though they lost, at least it was over. In the shade of the court change the game improved. His first net rush evolved into an overhead winner, a satisfying burying of the ball at Fritz's feet. An ongoing cross-court exchange with Mother followed.

Back and forth they went in a showcasing of consistency for the kids. When Fritz began sneaking sideways at net, showing his overeager poaching intention, Alex raided his alley with a down-the-line winner. The statement made, he settled into a mindless calm that is the tonic of tennis.

Alex's civility toward his partner shortly turned into something of a crush. She was a competitor despite the enormous wealth of her stepfather. Her pigtails banged soundlessly on her shoulder blades, and during her serve Alex twisted at net so as not to miss the way she hitched her second service ball out from underneath that mysterious underwear arrangement. At court changes, Melissa looked up at him yearningly, her pupils constricted to acute pencil dots in the summer light. He found himself chanting to her, "Right here," and "Always be closing," and "Here's where we stick it to Mom." They lost 6–3 but won the next set handily. Afterward it was decided that they would return to Totem Point for refreshments.

The New York financial papers had deemed Mr. Phillips a corporate "visionary," and true to form he had named his summer home Albion. A blend of domestic and imported seashells made up the driveway. The pink ones were from Bermuda, the white ones came from right here on the island. Alex wondered if Mr. Phillips would be home. For all he knew the man was tucked away upstairs or in some other vastly expensive apartment in New York. The man had his own plane, and if you owned a company he had his eye on, he'd eat it for lunch.

She led him into the kitchen.

"Well," she said, perched on a stool. "That was fun, wasn't it?"

"It was," he said. "I can't believe how good those two are."

"Isn't it wonderful," she said. "They can really hit the ball now."

A servant came in and began cleaning out the microwave.

"If you had your choice," she said, "would you call me Anne or Mrs. Phillips?"

Embarrassing, but that was how it was with the wealthy. They had no shame. Totally unselfconsciously, they delivered these extravagances at the feet of their guests.

"I avoid that dilemma by calling you nothing at all."

From a cabinet she pulled out a bottle of gin and stirred their drinks. The servant dropped an enormous block of foie gras and crackers before them. She smelled of so many things. She smelled of lime and gin, of liver and sweat, and money. Alex had to resist an urge to grab her waist. It was the secretly seething malcontent brewing somewhere beneath her well-kept frame that he wanted to touch, and in the air was a hint of an affair but not the blood. She would make him do it, and if he did, it would be an angry thing. He would lay her down. He would make her pay for overstepping the line of age, and it wouldn't be all *his* transgession either. It would be mostly hers. He allowed himself a sadistic fantasy involving the lifting of a tennis dress in an upstairs guest room. The maid disappeared from the kitchen. That left Melissa and Fritz in the neighboring room on the other side of the swinging doors. Were they a deterrent to a great kitchen pressing, or did the lonely drone of the television set signal the on-slaught of slumber party groping, an example to be followed?

"Do you like this part of the island?" she asked.

This was the mosquito-infested bay side with no surf. He had never liked it out here. The beaches were thin, and getting thinner. The people who bought and built out here were stupid. Suddenly, he realized he was getting drunk off his first drink.

"A few more hurricanes and there won't be any beach left here," he said.

"That's what they say," she sighed.

"Then another storm comes and your Totem Point goes."

"Ghastly, what Mother Nature can do. She is just *so* cruel to homeowners."

"Isn't she, though, but won't it be weird when your back lawn starts collapsing and Melissa has no house to inherit?"

"Ah, that's where you're wrong. You see, my husband can turn back the tides of nature."

"How's that?"

"He plans to build the retaining wall of all retaining walls. It may not be pretty but we'll survive. I didn't know you had a mean streak, Alex. Why are you trying to ruin my after-noon? Besides, by the time the wall crumbles you, and if you ever have any children, all of you will be dead."

"And so will you," said Alex.

"That's right, so drink up. Shall we make a toast?"

"To the lust of the goat," he said.

"To the glory of God."

She made him another drink. This was getting festive and scary. It was early yet to start drinking. His rule was he didn't mix his first until the sun was at least a thumb's width away from the sea, but here it was hazing over at four-thirty and he was holding another glass of gin. His knees were weak and his bowels loose with exercise and alcohol. Across the counter her face colored to an almost youthful hue of a college co-ed, a temporary condition, he was sure. She walked around the counter and stared out the window at the bay. Was this a signal for him to creep up on her from behind? Ice from his gin and tonic crashed against his teeth. That was it. Two drinks was appropriate, a civilized event with an interesting older woman. A third would be . . . He was not sure what a third would mean. But she was back beside him now at the counter, her body angling toward him, her hair flipped to one side.

His mother would be leaving Mr. Rittenhouse's funeral. He pictured her abandoned in Boston, standing on a hill of shimmering asphalt with a view of church steeples stabbing the sky.

He walked to the sink and rinsed out his glass. Overhead a toilet flushed. The beast, the homeowner, the great trader of companies and wives was home after all, or perhaps it was only the maid?

"I need to go to the bathroom," he said.

"You go through those swinging doors into the hallway and take a left," she said.

On the couch Fritz and Melissa were a jumble of sneakers and limbs so wrapped up in their mutual mugging that they took no notice as he passed.

"Stop that," he said.

But he had made a wrong turn. Instead of the hallway he

found himself in a giant living room filled with distressed furniture and exposed rafter beams. Various corridors led off into uncharted areas of the house. A criminal, drunken sneakiness came over him. He hated this house, and it suddenly occurred to him that he was not above stealing from it. Perhaps he'd come back during the winter and plunder the place, but for right now what he would give for a back patio door and a hidden piss in the bushes. Instead he plunged down a windowless hallway hung with African hunting shields. He stopped, turned, listened for the sea, but there was no surf on this side of the island, and taking his anger out on himself, he opened the nearest door.

From behind his desk Mr. Phillips took off his glasses.

"Well," he said.

He was bald. The man had never had much hair to begin with, but now he had taken it all off.

"Hi," said Alex. The study smelled of stale cigar smoke, shaved wood, and bourbon. On the wall behind the skin of Mr. Phillips' head was another skin, that of a gazelle next to a model ship within a magnum wine bottle.

"I've been carving," said Mr. Phillips.

"I'm sorry to interrupt. I'm trying to find my mother."

"Oh, but instead you got my wife."

"No, you see I got a little lost. I'm trying to find the front door so I can pick up my mother. She's at the airport."

"Did you have a good game of tennis? I thought I heard something about tennis."

"It was great. Those kids can really hit."

"Good," said Mr. Phillips. "That's what we send them to camp for. Don't you want to know what I'm carving?"

"Whatever it is I'm sure it's relaxing. I mean for a busy man like . . ."

"I'm carving a wooden bust of my soon to be ex-wife, and I've been drinking. I've been carving and drinking."

"Are you doing something degrading to her image?"

His laugh filled the study.

"Well, yes, as a matter of fact I am. Do you want to see it?"

"No thank you."

"Alex, do you like your job? I mean, do you feel that currency trading has any financial integrity whatsoever?"

"Not particularly, sir. I mean, sometimes it's a useful tool for hedging risk, but the more I look at it, the more I wish I hadn't left the law. It's mostly speculative stuff. You know, one man's loss is another man's gain kind of a thing."

"You're right," he said, and now he had swung around from behind his desk and was approaching.

"After Labor Day I want you to give my office a call. You understand. My office, you call it. We're going through a little shake-up right now, and I'll find you something worthwhile."

"Thank you," said Alex. "That's really very kind of . . ."

"Don't mention a thing."

"Mr. Phillips?"

"Yes, Alex?"

"Is there a bathroom nearby I could use?"

She was hugging herself at the window. The afternoon haze had burned off into the clean, sharp light of early sundown.

The wind had picked up, and the water in the near distance held the texture of crinkled tin foil stretching to a smoother sheen out to the horizon.

"Your drink's on the counter," she said.

"Are you trying to get me drunk?"

"No, I'm looking for something to drink to besides divorce."

"How about tennis camp," said Alex. "Let's drink to that."

"To tennis camp," she said, turning to face him.

"To getting your money's worth," he said.

"I did, didn't I," she said. "Or I guess *he* did at any rate. Not that the man could care one way or another."

For a moment her future flashed before him. She was emerging from her psychoanalyst's office on the Upper East Side of Manhattan readying herself for a late ladies' lunch and another round of legal proceedings with her lawyer. A fall divorce in New York, well, there was nothing dramatic in it really. Alex saw her in dark sunglasses walking the wealthy circuits of the city fortified with a giddy sense of temporary freedom. Perhaps she would buy a convertible.

"I think your husband just offered me a job."

"So here comes the monkey see monkey do financial routine."

"Are you testing your range?" he asked.

"How do you mean?"

"I mean, how old are you?" he asked her.

"Old enough to be your mother's youngest sister."

So that was it. She had been using him to gauge just how much youth she might still absorb. But their moment had passed, and as if to illustrate the point, she threw a black cardigan sweater over her shoulders.

"This was really sweet of you, but I've got to go," he said.

"Where do you have to go, Alex?"

His mother's return flight was still an hour away, but the best lie is always closest to the truth, and he gave it to her.

"Oh," she said. "Well, give her my best, will you?"

The driveway was a miasma of pink and orange in the setting sun, and the cool early evening wind coming in off the bay made him shudder and feel naked and cold in his whites. But his mother's Jeep greeted him like a friend, and getting inside he breathed out and stared down at the sand on the floorboards. When he looked up, he found a lone woman receding from his view. She was leaning against the doorway squinting at him through the sun. But the pull, the whine of reverse had already cast her in its undertow, and it was only an empty headrest his arm wrapped itself around as he steered clear of the cars in the driveway.

The Fixers

There was once an ad man, a journalist, and a junkie, and they all lived and breathed like fleas in the coat of New York City. One day the ad man walked out of his office and onto a midtown avenue. It said, here. Here in the city of use where the flags of the hotels and clubs fluttered their sheets above his head, here he had a choice. Today he had a choice, voices to listen to, to weigh, and pausing on the street he felt an offering in the air. It was a clear electric blue day in April. His lover, she mingled in that thrilling corner of his heart that still wanted to destroy himself, to make himself an early grave. His lover and her drugs, there was that, or home to his wife. His choice. He did not hate his wife. He loved her in the way one might love and fear a teacher. One day they had married to end a fight. Now they were husband and wife. Lover or wife? How many times has the question been poised on a set of wet lips for the first time in creation? But he was a free man, wasn't he? And in the scheme of things Charlie Way was a lucky man. He was young and working on the

Gillette campaign. It was the Best a Man Can Get. Good work, lucrative work, but like a lot of people in the twilight of their twenties, Charlie felt his was the success of an impostor. The Best a Man Can Get. He saw the steely grays, the minted teal freshness and aquamarines of the new line, so painfully focused grouped for maximum brand approval. Sure, he had stolen some color combinations from the new warm weather NHL expansion teams, but so what. That old mantra, the Best a Man Can Get, he was giving it a face-lift, a new meaning that had met with such overwhelming approval it seemed only natural to celebrate. Drugs or wife? The competing pressure systems on this clear banner day of advertorial triumph muddled his mind. The street did not help. It was a medley of after-work sneakers on beefcake pantyhose and sirens. His day had been too busy for lunch, and now the beckoning cherry light of the overhead Sbarro pizza lamps shone down on the toppings like a Christmas offering. Sbarro pizza. It said, here, come in here, and though he knew it was going down, Charlie Way could not see the sun setting anywhere at all.

In his trench coat like the others, with his thinning blond hair like the others, and briefcase that held the work of the impostor, he stood on the street thinking of Eve like no other. He still wanted to alter his life, see what would happen to it if he tried to throw it away, and on the perimeter of Times Square he waited for a sign. Fuck it, he'd go home. It was Thursday. He'd wait until Friday. He was making the right move. He'd go home and walk the dog. He knew the other way, Eve's way, was the wrong way, but that's what he liked about it, and how was one to reconcile that? He disappeared into the subway.

On the same day as Charlie was making his choice, a journalist was waiting for a story. He worked in his apartment alone, and his mind was thrilled by trends and the current goings-on of urban men and women. He made a living as a freelancer, that is to say, he hustled. He scooped up music, fashion, suicides, current events that, if one thought about it, represented something in society, and he put the loose ends together so that his readers could understand them generally, so that they might be made sense of as a trend. Eric Fogleman, he was a well-respected young generalizer, and it didn't hurt that he had an agent with a tongue like a wet whip. He did not need to look up the word "zeitgeist" in the dictionary anymore. It was the royal "we" of trend reporting where he had made his mark. For instance, he had broken the "cocooning" story.

"We are staying home and ordering out more and more these days," Eric had written.

He was tall and chiseled-looking, and though God had not granted him the kind of looks he seemed to claim he deserved, he had little trouble getting laid. All day long one could see just how finely toothed the comb was that had passed through his hair. He groomed himself as a man who looked like he knew what was going on right now, at this very moment in time, and he cultivated this look so as to capitalize on story pitches that would lead to work, money, and fame. Once he had even been interviewed on *Sonya Live*. Currently he was working on a story about heroin use among a young educated class of people in New York, and he felt the story meant something about an entire generation in despair.

Though Charlie and the journalist had never met, they happened to live in the same building, and they shared an interest in a woman.

That woman, she was a little bitch, and waking, she found there was something wrong with her soul. It was nothing new for Eve. The room seemed gassed by a sad late afternoon sun. She sat up in bed feeling the mis-invitation of the city greet her with its own personal melancholy. The reap-what-you-sow principle, it was getting a little belated in her life not to have recognized its ruling principle. She was filled with a petulant whining that was irresistible to men like Charlie. She whined a lot. Not on the surface because it was too pretty, but somewhere more deeply epidermal, one wanted to slap her, right across her porcelain junkie face with its pin-pointed eyes. She never left Manhattan. If she left Manhattan, her world would very nearly be over.

But what is it that has already been said about dishonesty in a woman—that it can almost always be forgiven? Charlie could always forgive Eve. Her smooth, finely shaved calves, the bathing oils, the brush strokes of conditioner that glistened in soft black hair. Before she went out to score there was her nightly tub and six or seven glasses of sweet dessert wine, or the whiskey sours she sweetened with five seconds of sugar poured from a stolen restaurant dispenser, the cotton between her toes, the red polish and the waxes, the sighs of resignation and boredom, frustration, and the half English-isms she had the pretension to pout out even to herself in the tub. Life was so hard, and junk so easy. Or was it the other way around? She did not know. She wished she could tear her addiction out with the same zeal of self-loathing she used to wax her bikini line. But she was born into the wrong time because she could have made someone a shiningly devious wife and lived out a relatively harmless alcoholic life in a well-curbed suburb, but she couldn't.

As she stepped out onto the street the stable of men in her life percolated in her mind. Tonight Charlie was a prominent one because he had not called. The weather, cusped between spring and summer, reminded her of his fair hair in her lap, and as she walked her neighborhood street, she wished he had called. But he hadn't, not for a while, and since she was one of those women who had one of those relationships with the telephone, his not calling was naturally of interest to her. Eve was wearing a woolen fire-engine-red cocktail suit that had belonged to her grandmother. Its mink collar caressed the back of her neck. Someone had left a bottle of cassis in her apartment so she had a nice little drunk on. She felt wonderful and in the periphery of her mind the conglomerated attention of men hovered like servants, or were they angels fanning her self-esteem? She felt extremely pretty on the front end of her drunk. In fact, as she stood waiting for a cab, she saw herself as the wealthy wife of a Phoenician maritime trader with a husband of means out at sea. Tonight she knew where she was going, and she understood the price of what it would be, and she did not need to be reassured of why she was going because she did not ask it, and how many people can say that at the outset of a New York evening?

She hailed a cab. There was barely any wind, but what there was brushed against her face with the textured embrace of a flower petal. Was it the encroachment of summer heat or the residual exhaust of an extinguished rush hour? It was difficult to tell. Opening the taxi door, she looked overhead at the intermittent coral pink clouds that spat out along a diluted blue sky. It was a weak sky, thought Eve, meek and ready to be taken over by the night.

At Rivington Street she stepped out into Spanish drug dealerdom. With the sun racing up the street at her, she looked like a stop sign in her red dress but who cared? She felt alive, and as for her friends? They had slipped away from the matter at hand, from what they needed. Their lives were not about a moment anymore. That is what she told herself standing on the street alone, that was the difference, the moment, she still had hers and they did not. There was a bodega on the corner and walking inside to buy cigarettes, Eve thought to herself what were these places? The store sold to the drug trade, and she felt the oppressive specificity of needs it served, the idle chrome meat slicer, the butane refill canisters, the cut-rate cigarettes, Joy and bleach and other miscellaneous needle-cleaning detergents. Even the empty Laundromat across the street with its motionless little holes stood at an attentive standstill, operable only for the washing of money.

"Baby, baby," said Big Bob, coming around a corner. "I've been waiting for you."

"Hi," said Eve.

"And going to get higher."

The dealer's eyes stood hatched at attention.

"There's this guy I want you to meet," said Big Bob.

"I don't fix. This guy sounds like he fixes. He's got this nice contaminated syringe and a rusty pecker that doesn't . . ."

"Oh man, Eve," said Big Bob. "It's like how many times do I have to bump up against your paranoia."

"What would you do without paranoia, Bob?" asked Eve. "Think about the coffee costs it cuts."

"I know, this place is a hard nut," he said. "I couldn't believe it. I got here in my brother's van this winter . . ."

It was Big Bob's van story. She had friends who were worse, who repeated themselves more often. Everyone did it, and some stories one could listen to a thousand times over, but the burden of Big Bob's winter van tale was that it illustrated the transitive power of debt. Big Bob owed his brother and Eve owed Big Bob. The transitive principle. It was pitiful. This life was pitiful, and inside her dead grandmother's suit pocket she balled up her little hand in rage.

"Fine, let's go see him," she said.

". . . so cold I thought my balls were going to fall off, and my brother's van was in the city's hands . . ."

"Bob."

"Cool, you don't fix, right, that's OK. He can work with that, I guess. He's just a guy I need you to meet."

They walked over to Houston, crossed it, and moved onto Avenue B. The beginning of that street with all its hitching street barter and kinetic confrontations and greetings sickened her. It was a sentimental world these men inhabited with their spiking drug-fed emotions and dramatic bullshit. They walked on, Big Bob nearly a paternal figure now, his sweat-tinged bulk pulling her along. On the corner of Eighth Street a man on a raised scaffolding was giving a Catholic church a new coat of yellow paint. Big Bob crossed himself.

"I didn't know we were that way, Bob," said Eve. "I thought you would have saved that for your basic mother-worshiping Spanish coke dealer, you know, bags on Saturday, church on Sunday?"

"Who the fuck do you think you are? Joan of Arc. Miss Beacon of the Eternal Light," said Big Bob, pulling up short. "You're down to me, baby. But it's like I can't get that through your pretty little head, and it's *really* pissing me off. You're down to me five bags and a favor, you know what I'm saying? That's just a fact. The fact. Five bags and a favor. I don't even have to *be* here right now. I could leave, then you'd come running looking for a party a little later on, but what would happen if I say to Julio, 'Julio, there's that bitch who's fucking you because she's fucking me?' You know what I'm saying? And then it's pop-goes-the-weasel for miss spoiled junkie bitch. You're in a carpet, and they've pawned your cute suit. Some other fashion bitch comes along and buys your dress. She pulls it off the rack, and you're in a carpet. She says, 'Wow, this is a fantastic deal, these places are great . . .'"

"What kind of carpet?" asked Eve.

Have you ever followed anyone? From the dog run, Charlie saw Eve against the day, pressed in red before the yellow of the church, coming down the street in her sickness. Though she did not see him, he did, yes, he saw her, very much he did. He saw her, and his mind was wasted on her in a dream.

And from his view out the window, Eric Fogleman saw Eve too. He smiled and poured himself a drink.

The dog squatted next to Charlie and began to take a quivering shit.

"Oh, Ralph," said Charlie.

One night Charlie and Eve had walked together into a handful of snowballing evenings with people shuffling around some misconceived party with stamps on their eyes. Then came the loping home to his wife and the accusations and crying, the begging, the promises and degradation. But they did it again, for the last time, and a week after that, they got together when his wife was out of the country. When was it, Charlie wondered, that fun had slipped over into obliteration? When was it that this cycle had begun? Walking around New York rubbing himself out, pulling himself back together, rubbing himself out, pulling himself back together, crawling to work.

When Eve and Big Bob turned into his apartment building, Charlie tailed them inside. He did not feign surprise at seeing her and she did not register it. The elevator rose within a preordained coincidence. He gave Eve a kiss. Was that a look of submerged pleading, of desperation and yearning that flared her neck tendrils out at him, or was it her persuasive aquiline nose that shook him, that bored into his heart, dissecting his desires?

"Where are you going?" asked Charlie.

"I don't know," said Eve.

"I know you," said Big Bob. "You used to come around."

The dog, out front on the situation as usual, sniffed at Eve's crotch and then mounted her dress on raised forelegs.

"I was thinking of you today," said Charlie, removing the pet from Eve's skirt. "I was going to call you."

"But you thought enough is enough."

"Not really. I wanted to celebrate."

"Then why didn't you."

"I thought I'd call you tomorrow," he said.

"I think something weird is going to happen to me in your building, Charlie."

"Shut up, Eve," said Big Bob. "I don't move weirdness, it's not a commodity I value."

"I'm broke," said Eve. "And I don't know how to fix it."

There was no time left now. The elevator had arrived at his floor. His wife was home. He felt her there in the apartment, waiting.

"I'm pressing 'Door Open,'" announced Big Bob. "Do you want me to keep pressing 'Door Open'? Because I'm feeling . . . I'm getting ready to press 'Door Closed,' you know what I'm saying?"

Charlie paced the hallway, leaving the dog panting at the door. He did not want to go into his own home. The thought of Eve perched above his head in such mysterious circumstances poisoned any possibility for a pleasurable evening with his wife. He looked at the animal drooling on the rug and kicked it.

. . .

"I hope this guy doesn't deal coke," said Eve. She had the uncanny ability of pushing one thing aside and picking up the other with a persuasive feminine bitterness that was difficult not to admire.

"Does he? Does he do that, Bob, does he move cocaine?"

"No," said Big Bob as the elevator door opened. "He moves information."

The door had been left open, and walking inside, Eve was confronted by an angelfish swimming the vivid blue waters of a computer screen.

"Come in," said a man sitting in the middle of a white couch. On top of a glass table and fanned out like a tightly cropped hand of playing cards were the covers of various fashionable magazines. Big Bob walked into the kitchen and helped himself to a beer.

The apartment was a large white box with high tin ceilings. Marooned in the middle of this emptiness was a bed. The curtains were white. There were off-white pine floors that smelled of a recent scrubbing. It was not unlike an art gallery without any work on the walls, and in the gaping space Eve experienced an intense wave of urban agoraphobia. Outside and softened by the rising stories of the building, came the distant snarls of a dog fight.

"You've got a nice place here," she said.

"Thank you," said the man. "I work hard."

"You do?"

"Yes, I do. In fact I'm rarely here."

"Really, where are you?"

"Working."

"That's nice," said Eve.

His eyes were hazel with disorderly spangles of white, as if a constellation of stars had exploded in the irises. Everything else, his apartment, his body, his close-fitting clothes had their place, and his black stereo which ran halfway up one white wall looked incredibly expensive.

"You must work really hard," said Eve.

"She doesn't fix," said Big Bob from the kitchen.

The man stood up. He had creased white chinos and a black turtleneck partially opened by a rounded zipper-pull. He walked over to his stereo and pressed a button. A door slid open and flattened inside the disc well was a bag of heroin.

"This whole CD phenomenon is such a conspiracy," he said, taking the bag out. "You know, over the years my record collection has grown into something of a library, and then they come out with the CD. You can't get anything on vinyl anymore. But my point is that when they first came out with the CD marketing promotions, they said you could throw the things around like Frisbees and nothing would happen. Total bullshit. The things scratch more easily than records, and if you ask me, the needle carries just as good a sound if your turntable's up to par."

"That's fucked up," said Big Bob. "You should do a piece on that."

"I was thinking about it," said the man, reaching for the stubble of a missing beard. "I was thinking about it."

A silence of solemn resignation for the music industry's culpability filled the room.

"I've only got a taste for you, Eve, just a taste," he said, shaking the powder onto the glass table.

The stars were coming out just above the balconied tree-tops of the park. A curtain blew into the room. Eve felt strangely in touch with the sounds below—the diminishing squelch of the basketball court, the back and forth continuum of a handball socking against a backboard wall, the intermittent cries of greetings and departures, and the peaks and valleys of the loaded car stereos building and fading into nothing. A damp air sat in with the fattening of that night charged with an unreadable meaning to her.

She snorted the heroin laid out for her on the table.

"Look," she said, coming up. "What the fuck is going on here?"

"That's entirely up to you," said the man.

"I'd love to hang around to watch things play out for themselves," said Big Bob from the kitchen. "But money never sleeps, you know what I'm saying, Eric?"

Without taking his eyes off Eve, Eric rocked back on the couch and reached into his pocket. He pulled out a silver money clip and peeled off three fifty-dollar bills.

"Thank you, Bob," he said.

"Wait a minute, Bob," said Eve. "I'm coming with you."

She tried to get up, but it took Big Bob two fingers to do what he needed to do.

"Sorry, Eve," he said. "Not unless you can come up with what you're down to me. That's just how it's been laid out."

"What?" said Eve.

"I'm a journalist," said Eric. "Don't worry about it."

"Yeah," said Big Bob. "And he never fucks his sources, right, Eric?"

"Right," said Eric.

"No names," said Big Bob.

"No names," said Eric.

They both laughed.

"You know, Bob," said Eric, "I thought we arranged for a spiker. As it stands now, the thing has less resonance, visually at least, without a needle."

Eve sat inside a warm womb of hatred. She felt cradled in an organically conceived outrage as soft as the touch of love, and with the same pull that is not unlike love, she wanted more of what was in Eric's bag.

"What do I have to do?" Big Bob put it to Eric. "Wrap your story up for you with a bow? I mean, I delivered. She's perfect. She's just what we were talking about, what you needed. So I'm sorry, you know, it's like she doesn't come with works included."

"Our deal was a fixer," said Eric. "That's all I'm saying. Next time, find one."

"Fine," said Big Bob and he was gone.

Eric stood up and cracked his neck.

"Do you mind if I make myself a drink?" he said.

"Do you have a cigarette? I lost my cigarettes," said Eve.

"I don't smoke."

"So what happens now?" she said. "We get to go to an ashtray switching restaurant where you have a lot of suck. Then you get to try and fuck me."

"The only reason we're pursuing this story at the magazine," said Eric, "is that in this age of irony, a return to dope makes such sense. Do you understand what I'm saying?"

He began to pace, to move through the empty room, warming up his pitch.

"It's representative of a kind of . . . a kind of . . . I don't know . . . a decadent nihilism. You are. You don't know it, Eve, but you are. You're representative . . ."

"Of what?" asked Eve.

"Oh, for God's sake," said Eric. "I tell you what I'm going to do. I don't smoke but I'm going down to the deli for your cigarettes. The beer's in the fridge. I'm only doing this because I'm a straight shooter, so if you want, you can walk, and if you want, you can stay. We can have a talk. We can go out to dinner and talk. Do you have a problem with that, talking? Is that really such a big deal?"

"Talk about what?" asked Eve.

"You," said Eric. "And what, if anything, you represent."

She straightened her skirt and tried to look representative.

For the longest time she stabbed at his stereo trying to get something to play, anything, but she couldn't figure it out. She pressed, she pointed, she stabbed at the black enameled buttons in a rising panic until suddenly a song came over the radio: "Hey . . . why don't you play . . . another somebody done somebody wrong song . . ."

Eve melted down, folding into its melody, holding the song against her breast and crying so that it might not go away.

. . .

Charlie Way's wife read Eric Fogleman's article in bed. It was a funny coincidence because in the story they had changed Eve's name to Liz, which was her name, Elizabeth Shankle, but sometimes people still called her Liz, which annoyed her no end. Up front the writer had made a big deal about changing Eve's name in order to hide her identity, and in the photograph Eve's hair hung down partially obscuring her face. In the photograph, Eve's teeth pulled on a piece of surgical tubing. She was captured bent over and jamming a needle home.

"Your friend, your little drug fuck?" she said, throwing the magazine at him and then sliding underneath the comforter. "I guess she finally stamped her foot hard enough that someone listened."

She was a small, beautiful bundle of a woman, and beneath the comforter she was crying and sinking into that almost reassuring constant of total-boyfriend-undertow. But he was not her boyfriend anymore. He was her husband. With the light from the bedside reading lamp cutting through the stitches of the comforter she could not believe he was actually her husband. She promised herself she would leave him. She swore an oath to avenge the spirit of her broken oaths to leave him, to make him leave. She made a very cold deal with herself.

"We never did anything with needles," said Charlie.

"That's comforting, honey," she muffled through the blanket. "Let me tell you, that really makes me feel like frying you an egg in the morning."

Charlie sat erect, jolted by the currents of infidelity laying a deadly grid upon the system of their bed. He knew a lawyer who knew a lawyer who'd get the divorce over quietly, quickly, and with as little mess as possible. Rationality in the face of panic, it was a male virtue, but there was no escaping the article on his lap. It was a public offering to the negligence of his desire, which as he thought about it, was the creeping endgame of his life. The photograph had an industrial strength tint of green and bore its black negative cropping, which, in the business, was considered raw. The prose spoke of "negative social synergies forged out of the meaninglessness of a headlong consumer society." According to Eric Fogleman, a new lost generation, a subculture of well-off kids, had cropped up. In another time, the story went, these young adults would have become leaders of their generation, but for various reasons they had opted out of a society they could no longer "negotiate." That was the word he used, and the writer made it clear that he had been there, had ventured to the edge of that world only to come back to report on it. Flanked by an Absolut ad and his own firm's L'Oréal spread, the Eve of Charlie's life and the Eve of those pages seemed forged in some basic discrepancy that tagged itself to the basement of his heart and blew an evil wind through the shutters of his mind.

"I'm sorry," he said to his wife.

"That's just never going to be enough anymore," she said, turning off the lights.

That winter Charlie walked through a falling snow to Eve's funeral. It was held in the freshly painted Roman Catholic church. Her parents had refused to identify the body because, they said, it ceased long ago to be the body of their child. On the stairs of the church he turned and gazed out at the stripped trees bowing to the winter wind. Then he faced the doors of the church. They said, here you are, here, come in here and welcome, welcome to the world, and though he scanned the magazines and papers afterward, there was no follow-up story, there was no obituary, there was no news at all.

How Much for Ho Chi Minh?

Shall we begin with the weather? Let's. The weather in this country made Richard want to streak, just take it all off, but he couldn't. He was in a government car. These ministry officials made Richard want to scream, but he could not scream. Face, apparently it was important not to lose it. The overarching authority of this city made Richard want to hide. But he could not hide. He had a job to do. The futility of his assignment made Richard want to cry. But he could not cry. He was in Hanoi, and he had to keep it together.

"So, Hung," said Sarah to their translator. "What happens in Hanoi on a Saturday night?"

They were an entourage of five packed into a black Soviet sedan. In the car was Richard and his girlfriend Sarah, a driver, Hung, and an anonymous Ministry of Information official who wouldn't give Richard his card. Hung cranked his neck in measurement of Sarah's question. What to do on a Saturday night? It was a dangerously open-ended proposition that dangled in the car for quite some time. The prudence and wariness of these people, it made Richard want to drink.

"My wife and I," replied Hung, "we take a walk by the lake."

"Really," said Sarah. "You paint such a romantic landscape. He never does that with me. You know what he does with me? He drags me to a decadent American rock and roll concert and then he comes home too drunk to . . . well, you know, Hung."

Hung was a thin, capable young man assigned to Richard in the spirit of generational compatibility. The color of his skin approached that of flypaper, and the five languages he spoke fluently made Richard feel slothful, blustery, and undisciplined.

"Do you like American music?" asked Sarah.

Hung turned his head away from the American couple and spoke to the driver in Vietnamese. He did not answer.

"It was a simple yes or no question, Hung, but I'm sorry if I offended you."

"No, you have not offended me," said Hung.

"Good," said Sarah.

Sarah asked Hung to ask the driver if it were OK to put in a cassette tape. The request was granted.

"Do you carry many of these recordings with you?" asked Hung.

"Yes," said Richard. "Vietnam is a wonderful country, but I'm afraid I don't have much of an ear for her music. It has no bass. I wonder why that is?"

"And they are of the modern American variety, your cassettes?"

"Well, sometimes Scoop can get rather sentimental," said Sarah. "Scoop, that's right, Hung, it translates roughly to 'he who digs his own grave.' Sometimes I come home and catch him playing 'California Dreaming.'"

" 'California Dreaming,' this is not a modern song?" asked Hung.

"It is commonly referred to as a golden oldie," said Richard. "I like to play them sometimes."

The cassette tape thundered into its opening number. Hung winced. Juvenile American exhibitionism, Hanoi was asking for it.

"Hung," said Richard. "I've got an idea. Why don't the two of us start a gossip column. A gossip column is what this town needs, more star power, less paperwork."

"Scoop here already misses Liz Smith," said Sarah.

"I read in the newspaper there is a beauty contest tonight," said Hung, not one to stray dangerously far from the spirit of any conversation.

"Really," said Sarah. "Scoop thinks Vietnamese women are as pure as raindrops on a water lily."

"Well, they *are*," said Richard. "Hung, isn't it true that the emperors in Hué had their tea made from raindrops gathered by maidens of the Imperial court who floated around in ponds full of water lilies?"

"This is indeed how one of our legends is told, yes," said Hung.

"Delicate, but disgusting," said Sarah. "I'm glad to see Vietnam has moved beyond such exploitative feudalism."

"My country is changing, forever there is change," said

Hung above the music. "Now we follow a path of openness in trade and business, but step by step."

"Step by step," said Sarah.

"Step by step," said Richard.

Step by step, it was the government line, a chorus to a never-ending song. The driver glared at them in the rearview mirror. Mr. Ministry of Information pulled out a small notepad.

Hanoi scared him. Like most Americans who broke the law, who jaywalked and experimented with drugs, who trespassed and did battle with the Department of Motor Vehicles, Richard saw himself as an essentially law-abiding citizen. But here, over his head in Hanoi, he felt as if his every fuck-up, past and present, stood before an omnipresent People's Committee. Luckily it was dusk, and with his first working day behind him along with several shots of joint-venture vodka, he walked the streets temporarily at ease. It was six o'clock on a Saturday in August of 1992. Shades of secondhand grays lent the wide boulevard a state-sponsored air of respectability while the smaller side streets teemed with the arrhythmic banging of crouched metallurgists. A man with no legs sat before a scale, and Richard grossly overpaid the invalid to weigh himself. In kilos, the whole thing was a mystery he did not care about.

Beside him a group of men were playing badminton. Was that the desk clerk at his Government Guest House? Or maybe it was that other guy, the assistant to the Deputy Minister of Foreign Affairs, the one who had forgotten to ask

for his lighter back. Or maybe it was that . . . it was no use
. . . Richard watched the shuttlecock arch back and forth,
and imagining the feathered bird was a hypnotist's pen, he
lapsed into a half sleep as the men in flip-flops danced shirt-
less in the summer street. Back and forth, back and forth, it
was a light game played by thin men in a heavy air.
Motorbikes and cyclos carrying live passengers and the dead
eclectic wears of Asian commerce weaved to miss the game.
But now the players had spotted their exotic spectator and
someone tapped him on the shoulder. It *was* the desk clerk.

"You play?" asked the man.

All the Guest House employees right down to the maids
had been trained by the East German Stasi, and it was no
state secret that the rooms were bugged. Still, this was no
time for paranoia. The street was marked with a rose-colored
chalk that reminded Richard of his sister's hopscotch scrawl-
ings in Central Park. There was a kind of UN style bonhomie
in the air. A teenager put a Chinese racket in his hand. In
exchange Richard took a Walkman from his pocket and
showed the boy how to use it. Then he shook hands with his
team. The breakfast waiter from the Government Guest
House had teamed up with the front desk clerk, the one who
had had the last word on his slightly torn one-hundred-dollar
bill. He was a Guest House heavy, graying pleasantly, the
very picture of Zen, definitely a spy. That made two Guest
House employees. Richard did not recognize the others.

He found himself wobbling near the net where he could
take advantage of his one asset, height. But it was no good.
He was neither patient nor steadfast. He was a weak American man, a slave to his appetites, unable to disguise a thing.

Badminton with all its essential subtleties played to the elements of the Vietnamese character he lacked. Partially processed vodka burned his stomach. The shuttlecock began coming in double. The teenager squatted on the curb thoroughly overwhelmed by the power of the Walkman. Richard worried he might be spreading an infectious disease.

Between points he began to have disturbing surveillance fantasies. From his room, what might they have heard and passed along to higher channels? Well, besides Richard's list of questions which Sarah had demanded he read out loud and the little whimper of his single Hanoi ejaculation, there had been a fight. She had wanted to come along to the interviews that morning. He did not want her to come. Sarah was not a journalist. She was an artist. She installed installations and made "objects" in New York. He did not want to see her in the Ministry of Foreign Affairs. He did not want to see her in any ministry whatsoever. Her retort had been, fuck you, I've come all this way with you and I'm not missing out. She had a camera, and though Richard was on assignment for a magazine that ran no photographs, she assumed she had the right. They'd had it out while Hung waited downstairs in the car.

"It's just not *done* over here, OK," he had said. "You don't show up in these places with your girlfriend. I mean, it's fine if we're talking to Fat Hat in Saigon, and he's giving you a free plane ticket to Moscow and his 'trip for two on a one-way ride' routine, but Le Van Bang is a different story. This is Hanoi. I'm supposed to be a professional."

"And I'm the photographer, what's the big deal?"

"There's nothing to photograph. There will be teacups in a conference room with men in it."

Plenty of tea was right, so much tea that he began to sweat. Little raindrops fell from his armpits and by the third interview his white button-down shirt was a translucent embarrassment. The Deputy Minister of Information asked him if he had a fever. By then he was glad to see his girlfriend crouched with her camera in her least racy Kenneth Cole shoes documenting his futility. She even took a picture of him, notepad in hand, and what a wet T-shirt contest that was going to be. Looking down at himself, Richard could make out the lines of his nipples. But was Sarah not a comfort? Was she not a sunflower brightening these austere ministerial rooms with their hedged answers and razor-backed chairs?

Le Van Bang's office had lace doilies on the low-lying conference table and a rotating fan that circulated the hot air most efficiently. There was something secretive and serene about the office with its ocher-colored walls and chipped ceiling. Large French windows gave out onto a circular driveway, and on an opposing wall was a photograph of Uncle Ho poring over a map with General Giap. While Hung translated his questions, it evolved that Le Van Bang, the biggest fish of them all, was avoiding Richard's line of questioning and gazing at Sarah. The wise old geezer was charmed by her, bored with Richard. There then followed an artful one-eighty-degree rotation in the line of questioning so it was *she* who was being interviewed.

Pennsylvania was a large state, yes. No, not all of it was

considered the East Coast, though she herself was from the eastern part of the state. She had grown up on a farm but her father was not a farmer, no. They used to grow corn and wheat but not any more. Landed gentry? Well, that was a bit of an antiquated term, but her father did collect a nominal fee for the use of his land. How many dollars per square kilometer? You know, that was a very good question. It was an issue that was never openly discussed. A repressed family? Oh, that means ... Well, what should I say that means, Scoop? She looked his way for assistance and received none. No matter, now she called New York her home. Yes, the city was certainly an exciting cultural center but there was a great crime problem. Some of the Vietnamese in New York were indeed in criminal gangs. Yes, in Ho Chi Minh City there did appear to be a strong demand for pirated American music. As for that report about the rock and roll singer who advocated suicide in some of his songs, yes, that report was correct, but the minister must understand the singer in question was not necessarily representative of all Western music. Was he a symptom of a sickness? Well, yes, that was a fair enough statement. Potholes? She could understand the confusion. No, they were not made from explosive devices. They were disturbances in the road, small and sometimes quite large holes. But sometimes it did certainly seem as if a small bomb had gone off. How many centimeters wide on average? She could not accurately estimate, perhaps twelve. They were created from extremes in temperature and municipal malfeasance. Yes, New York needed fixing. It was nothing like Hanoi.

. . .

A cry came up from the badminton game. Richard had spiked one at the feet of the Guest House waiter. Preoccupation was improving his game. He'd found his niche at net after all. Now it was time for a blustery exit. Summoning the role of American imperialist poaching at net, he launched himself into the air and in an overzealous repeat of his last shot, missed the bird and snapped the net.

The next morning the telephone rang.

"OK, but why don't you order us some coffee," said Sarah. "We'll be down in a while."

Then she hung up the phone, rolled over, and sighed at the ceiling.

"That was Hung. He's in the lobby."

Richard groaned.

"Hung like a dog," he said. "It's Sunday. Why can't someone either help me out or leave me alone?"

"Get dressed," said Sarah.

"But we don't have anything scheduled for today."

"Get dressed."

They had planned a quiet guidebook-driven day to themselves centered around French food and a visit to Ho Chi Minh's mausoleum. The next round of interviews was scheduled for Monday, so what Hung was doing sitting at the breakfast table with his spindly legs tightly crossed was something of an annoying mystery.

"Good morning, Hung," said Richard.

"Good morning."

Hung ashed his cigarette and then took his head in both hands and cracked his neck. The waiters coalesced on the far side of the room in an incentiveless air of hostility. Tipping was not discouraged, it was prohibited. Sarah lit a cigarette and blew smoke Hung's way.

"Isn't Hung looking sort of dashing this morning," she said. "What's with the shirt?"

"And the jeans," said Richard. "Where'd you get those styling jeans?"

The waiter from the badminton game came by to take their order.

"Yesterday in the street? Good game," said Richard. "I like very much . . ."

The waiter pretended not to recognize him.

"He's probably pissed you snapped his net," said Sarah.

She turned to Hung.

"So, to what do we owe this Sunday morning visitation?"

Over their second coffee, the situation crystallized.

"What is the expression? Ah yes," said Hung. "Pocket change. The driver needs pocket change. The subsidies for gasoline were reduced last month, but the rise in price has, naturally, not yet been reflected in our ministry's paper-work."

It was not like Hung to criticize his ministry and Richard was at once disturbed and fascinated with this mild metamorphosis. Through the window he gazed out at the driver in the black sedan. Usually the man's face appeared cut from a coin. Now, on his day off, his eyes flickered like a lizard's tongue.

"The driver also says his niece was married last night," said Hung. "But I do not believe this for a fact."

"Fine," said Richard. "How much for a visit to the Ho Chi Minh mausoleum?"

"And after, a walk by the lake," said Sarah. "How much for a walk by the lake?"

A British woman they'd had dinner with the night before came into the restaurant and sat down at the table. She was doing advance work for a flooding conference sponsored by the UN. Sarah called her the "tea bag." Richard had made a drunken pass at her in the bar of the Metropole Hotel the previous evening. She had rejected him in a charming fashion.

"What is that disgusting expression you Americans created?" said the tea bag. "Oh yes, date rape. Last night I was date-raped by the UN's High Commissioner for Refugees."

Hung bowed his head. Then he reached for the tea bag's pack of cigarettes and took one. In that gesture Richard caught an essential transformation in Hung. The barrage of incessant Western free-market disclosure heavily laden with sexual nuance was like a pill slowly taking effect. This talk of nightclubs and date rape, the music, the jousting, it was all so indicative of the shape of things to come, Hung's forehead nearly touched the table. Richard continued to press.

"In dollars or dong, Hung? Let's begin there. The Ho Chi Minh Mausoleum followed by a walk by the lake. I'll pick up the picnic for you and the driver. But first we must come to a calculated currency agreement. U.S. dollars or Vietnamese dong?"

"Wait a minute, I want to meet the wife," said Sarah. "How much for the wife?"

"Stop," said Hung. "Stop, both of you. You must not talk of my wife."

"Hung doesn't get my humor," said Sarah. "He never has."

There was a long silence. The entire Government Guest House seemed poised on the brink of a great compromise.

"Dollars," said Hung. "But first you must go upstairs and collect your music cassettes. We must visit a friend of mine."

The friend called himself Zip. His apartment was a depot for the playing, recording, and copying of music, plus a bed. It was strange because from the street Zip's apartment was like so many others Richard had seen in Vietnam. There was the cheap concrete, the steel gate falling vertically to the ground, the Honda "Dream" motorbike parked inside. Zip's living room was his bedroom, and it appeared as if his kitchen doubled as a toilet. There was a guitar dubiously announcing itself as a Gibson, a floor of black cords, speaker wire, duct-tape, and a wall of stereos. In the back of the apartment there was one small window and through it Richard could see children splashing water in an alley. This alley, partially eclipsed by hanging laundry, did not give onto the main street. It was a back door alley that secretly meandered from house to house.

Zip smoked Marlboros, a good beginning. Since he'd been in Vietnam, Richard had given away nearly two cartons. Now he was sick of it. Standing in this recording shop, he felt it was a good time to take, not give. But perhaps his host had already sensed this. Fine, he'd take a Marlboro. This Zip was thin with a clammy handshake and black eyes.

"So what can I do for you?" asked Richard.

Zip was interested in a record that had come out in 1991. It was not only a fabulous record, but it had the distinction of having replaced a commercially disfigured pop star from the top of the charts. Richard had the tape in his possession along with a few others. Zip wanted them all.

"So *this* is what you do on your days off, Hung," said Sarah. "You broker music deals. I never would have guessed."

Hung was not amused. He kept his back pressed to the latched front door.

"You know," said Richard, "there's a law against this. It's called copyright infringement. I don't mind fucking over David Geffen, but you sell five thousand of these on the street and it's all in your pocket, not in the band's."

"Your tapes," inquired Zip. "Are they good recordings?"

"Well, they're not the digitally mastered mother of all frequencies, but yeah, they're pretty good. Some of the levels may be somewhat high, but . . ."

"Let me see one."

"Let you see one for what?"

"I just want to listen to it, okay. Then we can talk. You need a drink."

"Where'd you learn your English?" asked Sarah.

"My mother."

Zip barked something in Vietnamese, and Hung marched over to a small refrigerator. Richard was disappointed in Hung's edgy servility. Translator was playing butler now.

"Why, thank you, Hung," said Sarah. "Do you by chance have a lemon? I can smell the formaldehyde already."

Zip put on a pair of headphones with oversized black leather earmuffs. Then he squatted on his haunches for a listen. There was no hiding it; from the first inaudible chords, Richard could see the bliss move across Zip's face.

"So, Hung," said Sarah. "What kind of a percentage does he pay you?"

Hung said nothing. Even the great Vietnamese propensity for subterfuge and disguise could not hide the competing pressure systems that ripped through his conscience. A youth spent diligently climbing the Communist Party ladder. The textbooks and lectures on the evils of capitalist imperialism, and then to arrive at the beginning of real adulthood only to be greeted by this, Zip and the great Vietnamese money grab. The training, the rote learning, the discipline, it was all crumbling before the hidden god of profit.

"Hung, quick 'Teen Spirit' is a great song," said Sarah. "But it doesn't last forever. What kind of a percentage is he paying you?"

"No percentage."

"Well, what is your deal with this guy?" asked Richard.

"He is my wife's . . . not brother . . . what is it? He is my wife's cousin. He gives me five dollars for every piece of music he accepts."

"Oh, Hung," said Sarah, reclining on Zip's bed. "That's so pathetic. You've got to go for points on the net."

"Points on the gross," said Richard. "A friend of mine told me only suckers go for points on the net."

"Points? I do not understand," said Hung.

"It's called a cut, Hung," said Richard. "This guy is taking you."

"Taking me where?"

"To the cleaners," said Sarah.

"I do not understand."

Zip took off the headphones and surveyed the room.

"I do not need to tell you that this music is forbidden."

"What's forbidden?" asked Richard. "The music or you making money off copying it?"

"Your recording, why is it so sloppy?"

"Because I taped it before the illuminations of an American stereo for an audience of two, my girlfriend and myself."

"And you do not have the CD."

"I don't travel with CDs, Zip."

Zip put the headphones back on and changed tapes. Richard was torn, and so he walked over to his girlfriend. There on Zip's saggy bed, with a Saigon beer in her hand, oh, how luscious a market-savvy sight was that? They huddled in conference.

"So what do you think?" asked Richard.

"I think Zip's sort of a worm, but the music is great. The other thing is, I've always hated free concerts. Remember that time we saw what's his face in that stupid park, and you said, 'Nothing comes for free.' That show was awful."

"So what should I do?"

"Well, first off, I think he's bullshitting about the recordings. After all, it wasn't *you* who taped them, it was me. So it goes without saying, I get half."

"No you didn't. I thought I taped them."

"Action item two," she continued. "We're not doing this deal unless Hung gets points."

"Hung gets points," agreed Richard.

"Points or we walk."

They began making out furiously on Zip's bed.

"You know, Scoop," she said. "Sometimes . . . sometimes you're the man."

Hung never did get his points. Zip was too vicious a negotiator. Preying on their weakness for music, Zip said they didn't understand. It would be difficult to get some of these recordings even in Thailand. The state was opening up the country to the oil companies, yes, but they were still very gun-shy when it came to music. Zip said it wasn't a question of profit, it was a question of defying the state in the interests of rock. It was the "music has no borders" thing, that sentiment. Sure they bargained, but Zip's line was Hung didn't deserve a percentage, gross or net. Hung wasn't the one taking the risk on the sales end in a police state, nor was he bearing the cost of production. So they settled on adjusting Hung's finder's fee significantly upward.

As for Richard and Sarah, well, they walked out of that apartment and into that awful heat with a mind to visit Ho Chi Minh's grave with Zip's fifty-dollar bill between them, he holding one end of it, she tugging the other. Behind them walked Hung, his wrists held behind his back, his head bowed in compromise, or was it prayer? It was a quiet street in the hottest hour. A man lying in a perfectly still hammock waved, as the driver inched the car alongside them smiling a silver tooth.

"Happy?" asked Richard. "Are we happy now? Everyone is going to get married, rich, and have a thousand wives."

Hung got into the front seat of the car and for a moment the driver and translator peered out at the American couple standing there on the sparkling pavement looking down at President Grant. As for love? Well, it had risen again. It was present and accounted for, twinkling amid the dissemination of rock and roll, dancing to the soft pitch of an invisible gold sound.

Preexisting Condition

He was on his way to meet a troubled young lady he had fallen abruptly in love with in the hospital. It was the evening of April Fools', and outside the air was a thrill of broken promises. He found himself at the foot of a residential street. A dog straining against its chain barked as he passed in the rain. Shut up, he thought, shut the fuck up, you fuck. Shut it. He pushed his plastic patient bracelet up his forearm, stretching it into a tourniquet. Shortly he found he could no longer feel his hand.

At a highway overpass cars rushed below him in a calamity of motion he found unsettling to the sedentary shuffling and moody self-examinations that had been life in rehab. It was drizzling, and he considered turning back but instead stuck his head inside his sweater and T-shirt to light a cigarette. It was a move from his pot-smoking days. When he came up, he saw letters moving laterally in ticker-tape fashion. They were blurry little stars from the convention center, and they were moving behind a forest of leafless trees off to one side of the highway. He climbed down from the overpass and stood in the emergency lane shivering. He would have to cross the highway to reach the wood that led to the convention center. Perhaps it was the loneliest moment of his life. He had no friends here. He had no car. What he had was an as-the-crow-flies feeling of trespassing and his wallet. For a moment he closed his eyes and considered walking out onto the highway, but when he pictured this stupidity, he became so disgusted with himself he almost did it anyway. He checked his laces. Then he stood waiting for a gap in traffic.

One night in the smoking room he introduced himself. She had raven black hair and beguilingly smooth skin. Her eyes were spaced so widely apart, he worried about her brain. With their seatbacks facing one another, they blew smoke out their noses and played the name game. It was almost time for beddy-bye so they made it quick. She'd met his ex-girlfriend Lidia a handful of times in New York. They had friends in common but had never become friends themselves. No, she had never met Lidia's friend Gida. She had gone to boarding school with a cousin of his whose intelligence and verve he had always been drawn to. A close girlhood friend of hers was in turn a pal of a woman he had once briefly dated before Lidia. Dating was putting it politely. The affair had ended poorly for everyone concerned. She had been a groupie for a vaguely famous rock band he thought overrated. The name game segued into drugs. Their habits followed a similar road map. It was surprising they hadn't met. She'd lived on the East Coast all her life but for the last three years. Currently she was renting a house a few miles from the hospital. This was her third rehab. She loved cocaine.

Suddenly, impulsively, and with the brazen confidence of someone with very little to lose, he kissed her.

"Now what do we do?" she asked. "Fuck each other out of detox."

"I'm out of detox," he said.

"Good, you'll be able to take your time then."

It was a disciplined piece of clockwork lovemaking. Every other night they slept together. His room one night, no sex, her room the next, no sex, his room, and so forth. From eleven-thirty to eleven-fifty they hoisted one another's hospital gowns and fucked. By midnight they were asleep in their respective beds. Sex was banned in rehab, as was any "exclusive relationship." To keep the noise to a minimum, he put a pillow over her face at the appropriate moment. There was no birth control whatsoever. He pulled out. Afterward she douched. During the day they nodded at one another knowingly in the halls. It was a kind of love he'd never felt before. It wasn't particularly strong as it was accurate, and in its accuracy, there lay an honesty he was drawn to.

One night he walked into her room and was horrified to find that she smelled of gin.

"I can't believe you're drunk," he said.

"Yes," she considered. "I suppose I am."

He pushed her onto the bed, grabbed both her wrists, and smacked her.

"What the fuck do you think this is?" he hissed. "Boarding school? I can't believe you're drunk. This is a hospital filled with drunks. Fuck-ups, get it. We're all fuck-ups trying to figure out how it is we got so fucked up. You can't fool a fuck-up at his own game, Jean."

He slapped her again, twice, across each cheek. She took it with a blank self-abnegation that infuriated him. He raised his hand again.

"Get off me," she said.

"Fine."

He paced about her room.

"I'm going to tell Sarah," he said. Sarah was her group counselor.

"Sarah is one of the reasons I went out," she said. "Besides, narcs are not invited into my boudoir. Get out."

"No, I don't think so," he said. "I don't think I am going to do that right now. What are you going to do, scream?"

"Give me a cigarette," she demanded.

He opened her window and lit a cigarette for himself. It was a clear breezy night. Clouds slipped past a quarter moon, and at the far end of a nearly empty parking lot there sat a BFI Dumpster.

"Give me a cigarette."

"I only have one left," he said. "You think I'm going to give you my last cigarette?"

"Please, Ian," she whined. "Please. I really need a cigarette."

"Bum one at a bar."

She began to cry.

"I'm not going to do any more coke," she said. "The whole coke thing is over. I swear. I swear to God, but I'd rather be drunk than sit in this place again."

"Jean, booze is a gateway drug to coke, don't you get it?"

"Recycle that borrowed jargon on someone else," she said. "You're a portrait of a rehab robot."

"You will be dead soon. Your portrait is frozen. It's entitled 'lush.' "

Lighting his last cigarette he watched as she got out of bed and began to stuff clothes into a gym bag.

"In a week or so," he continued, "you'll be back to playing the coke whore. It will be your very last role, and I'm sure you'll be most convincing."

His face stung from her smack, and then there was a tussle to see who would first get to his rolling cigarette ember.

"The last shall be first, and the first shall be last," she said, sticking the filter in the middle of her mouth.

"Oh my God," he said. "A chapel talk from the coke whore."

He watched her greasy black hair flash in the moonlight as she packed.

"Where are you going to go?" he asked.

"There's a convention center about ten blocks from here. A bunch of insurance adjusters are in town. They're just dying for my company."

"Jean, look," he said. "Don't go. Just don't. Look, you can smoke my last cigarette. In fact, we can sit and smoke some more. I've got another pack in my room. Just for you. Just come back and we can smoke."

But she was already out the door.

. . .

It was a sick wood. Above him a plastic bag snared on a branch blew in the wind. Below the moist ground was an archaeology of alcohol, swollen with half-submerged bottles, stray sneakers, and beer cans. It was as if a caravan of death metal fans had encamped for some secret ritual of debauchery, and he half expected to find a body hanging from a tree. In the distance, rain drummed off the roofs of vehicles parked near the convention center. He went over his plan. Save Jean. Live with her, love her, keep her straight. In his arms he felt certain that he could extract her from her current degrading position. He ran for the parking lot but lost traction and fell.

"OK," he said. "Count to ten."

A Postal Service cover band was playing the cocktail lounge sporting matching red blazers and eagle patches. The television was turned to a silent hockey game. Out-of-town businessmen, still stuck to name tags, milled about the room. She was at the far end of the bar peering beneath a leather cup, playing liar's dice. She looked good. Her cheeks had color, and she had on a short black dress and a silver choker. He peered over her shoulder.

"Three fives," she said to a man whose beeper went off.

"Sorry, babe," said the man, standing up. He wore a full-length black leather coat with a fur collar. "You're lying, and I've got to go call Mommy."

"Whatever," said Jean. "But I hope it's what's his name. You know, Mr. Kilo-Cutter. If it is, tell him I know where *his* mother lives."

Ian Easley took a seat on the man's bar stool. It was hot from hours of sitting and drinking.

"Oh, Ian," she said. "Don't. Don't sit there. Am I really that contagious?"

"I thought I'd come by and check up on you," he said. "You know, see how you were doing?"

"I'm doing fine. People are really nice here."

"Good," he said. "I'm glad you're doing fine."

He gestured to the bartender.

"Don't, Ian," she said, taking his wrist. "Why do it? Why flush a month down the toilet?"

"I'm sorry, but there were two things I never envisioned. One was you, and the other was no you in a hospital with lots of Canadians in it."

The drink arrived and he raised his glass.

"To the Beast," he said.

With a whiff of her hand she knocked his drink onto the floor.

Ian pulled a credit card from his wallet, and finding his old barroom baritone ordered another drink.

"Elliot," she said to the bartender. "Elliot, don't serve this man."

Elliot, a healthy-looking blond of Scandinavian stock, bent underneath the bar and came up with a bronze medallion reserved for graduates of the program. It was the color of a penny and the size of a silver dollar. Engraved on the back Ian recognized the serenity prayer, "God, grant me the serenity . . ."

"I collect them," said Elliot.

"That's a pretty morbid thing to do," said Jean.

"You know what's even more morbid?"

"What's that?"

"You guys," said Elliot. "You guys don't even have one, so I can't serve you a free drink for a medallion, as is my custom. But if the man wants a drink, Jean, he wants a drink, you know what I'm saying? I can't say to the man, 'Hey, I'm sorry, drinking is bad for your liver.' "

"Drinking is bad for your liver," came a voice at Ian's back.

It was the man in the black leather coat. He had such shrewdly criminal features, Ian immediately felt inferior to him. He looked like a drug dealer in a Western.

"We've got to ride," he said to Jean.

"Already? I was just starting to feel cozy, James."

"Look, if you want to bring your friend along that's fine. We could use the company."

"How about a drink?" said Ian.

"No time," said James.

James was driving a silver Crown Victoria with various antennas and chrome side view mirrors that lent the whole enterprise the authority of undercover law enforcement.

"So," said James once they'd eased out onto the highway. "What do you do for a living?"

"I work for a theater," said Ian.

"That doesn't sound very lucrative, Mr. Easley."

"No, it isn't. In fact we've taken to stealing cars to finance some of our productions. Now I'm checking up on Jean here."

"You don't look like much of a car thief," said James.

"You'd be surprised what some people will resort to in order to put on *Lear* again. I guess it's a 'Reason not the need' kind of a thing."

In fact Ian's theater company did not steal cars, but around this man he felt the need to cultivate the criminal.

"What do you do?" asked Ian.

"I help manage risk."

"Fine with me," said Ian.

"You know anything about this city?"

"I know what state it's in."

"Yeah, well, that's a start," said James.

"I've been to the Phillips 66 across from the hospital," said Ian. "For cigarettes. Once I leave, I hope to never come back."

"You will," said James.

"Why do you say that?"

"Because your mother took one look at you and bought a whole shitload of insurance. If I was the Travelers, you know, the big red umbrellas. If I were they, I'd take a hit out on you."

"Jesus, James," said Ian. "You must think I have a drinking problem."

"Drinking problems are my specialty," said James. "Do you know what percentage of drunks nationwide touch down in this town for treatment?"

"I would suspect a lot, James."

"A surprising number is right, but what's even more interesting is the number of people like Jean here who take up semipermanent residence. What I do is check up on all the rehab dolls who thought they had gotten clean but are still residing in this state and are out drinking again. Jean here is my assistant."

"Yeah," said Jean from the backseat. "We're a team."

"I'm making a list. Then I report back to my employers and they cancel policies, get it?"

Ian turned to Jean. She was sniffing coke from a spoon chained to a vial. What a peccant little bitch she was. At first he had admired her choker. Now he took it as the sign of the devil.

"You don't have to watch," she said.

"I won't."

Their affair meant nothing to her now. It had been a replacement chemical, another endorphin, a temporary tenant subletting a room in her rented body. Now the anchor tenant had arrived. She had no need for him.

"Where are we going?" he asked.

"We're looking for a house in St. Paul," said James. "It's called the Home for Chronic Inebriates. Mr. Kilo-Cutter claims they're having a party tonight."

The highway ran straight for miles, coming at them black and flat.

"Are you covered?" asked James.

"How do you mean?"

"I mean," said James, "insurance-wise."

"Well, James, on that score, you're right. My mother did take one look at me. The insurance thing is in her hands. But I'm not covered beneath the red umbrella. I've got the blue shield to protect me."

"Good," said James. "I don't work for that particular outfit, so your secret is safe with me."

"I wouldn't take you for an insurance man, James."

"Well, that's because I freelance. I make sure that high-risk cases, you know, major-league liabilities, end for my employers. That's my job."

"How do you mean end? Do you put a hit out on them?"

"Have you ever heard of a preexisting condition?" asked James.

"Yeah, I have one. It's called alcoholism."

"Voilà," said James. "We're getting somewhere. I search out those with a preexisting condition that . . . let's see, how should I put this . . . a preexisting condition that has a nasty habit of flaring up again."

"So you're an insurance company bounty hunter slash private dick, wow," said Ian. "I'm really glad to make your acquaintance."

"Not to mention," said Jean, "a rugged individualist. James *works* for his living."

"Look," said James. "I save corporate America a pretty penny, and mind you, I'm compensated well for my job."

They turned off at an exit, and the lighted windows of St. Paul began rolling by in silence.

"I know everyone with a preexisting condition in a fifty-mile radius," said Jean. "Minus some of the senior citizens, that is."

"Do you know how much it costs a company," said James, "a company like the Travelers to put one of you guys through a six-week program?"

"Jesus," said Ian. "Aren't we repeating ourselves a little? Can we talk about something else? How about architecture? How about music?"

Ian spun the radio dial all the way left. Jazz filled the car. It was the sound of men playing bridge with their instruments.

"Could you believe that Postal Service band?" said Jean.

"Those guys should play the hospitals," said Ian. "It would be a better venue for them."

"The post office is turning into a shooting gallery," said Jean. "They're killing each other. COD style."

"How much farther is it?" asked James.

"It should be coming up here on the right."

"Are we going to a cocktail party?" asked Ian. "Because if we are, if we're going to a cocktail party, I think I'll stay in the car."

"Here it is," said Jean. "Open up your stockings, everybody. The Chronic Inebriates are pulling out the plugs."

They came to a four-story clapboard house on a residential street a few miles from downtown St. Paul. There were cars parked on both sides of a winding suburban road, and on the lawn outside this house two men with motorcycle helmets were breaking beer bottles over one another head.

"Oh God," said Ian. "Please save me from this shit."

On each floor people could be seen dancing and drinking, cavorting and bending over mirrors.

"The thing about the Home for Chronic Inebriates," said Jean, lifting a pair of binoculars, "is you can only live or party here if you've been through the program ... Ouch, this is a good one. I see what's his face, the rail welder for Amtrak."

"What's he drive?" asked James.

"That black Lincoln over there. He's checked in at least five times."

"He wasn't on my floor," said Ian.

"Shut up," said James, taking down the Lincoln's plate number.

"Yep," said Jean, eyeing the cars. "It's the medallion squad, and a medallion party wouldn't be a medallion party without Bancroft. He checked out of St. Mary's less than a week ago."

"Yeah?" said James. "What's he driving?"

"His mother's Jetta."

"The green one."

"Yeah, the green one."

"Good," said James. "That guy's a liability."

"Major league," said Jean. "Complete lights-out drunk. I heard he once blacked out his wedding proposal."

"Who else?"

"Lapsly," said Jean.

"I thought he'd been clean for years?"

"He's the blond guy on the third floor with the stupid shirt," said Jean. "I can't see what he's drinking."

James got out his own set of binoculars.

"Whiskey."

"Poor Lapsly," said Jean.

"What does he drive?"

"I don't know."

"I thought you were running the car part of this operation."

"Sorry, James, Lapsly's an old friend of mine. Can't we cut him off the list?"

"Leniency," said James, "is not in the contract."

"Come on, James."

"Yeah, James," said Ian. "Have a heart."

"Friends," said James, "tonight we're taking down names and numbers. Now let's get to it."

For James it wasn't a bad night of work. After the initial reconnaissance, he sent Jean into the party for deeper "fieldwork." She came back with a gold mine. It turned out the Chronic Inebriates paid dues in order to assure collective maximization of their booze-buying potential. Jean managed to steal the clipboard. Out of the two dozen dues-paying members, James explained there was a high probability that at least ten were covered by his various employers.

"So," said James. "Where to now?"

Earlier in the evening Ian had touched that corner of himself that needed a drink, but now there was nothing he wanted more than to be back in his hospital bed. He could feel Jean in the backseat chewing on her jaw, putting out her snarled coke vibrations. He sat back in his seat and sighed. This was slavery. He was in the middle of a night of slavery people mistook for a good time. A good time, it was sad to see how people chased it, beating up their minds, mangling their hearts, chasing their tales around and around until they were left at the bottom of some filthy drain of their own creation. He'd come to save Jean, but a poor swimmer should never try to save the drowning.

"To the hospital," said Ian.

"Yes, James," said Jean. "To the hospital."

Perhaps, thought Ian, I am cured.

Marriage Is Murder

For Eoghan and Libby

If it sounds like this honeymoon ski vacation was not my idea, bingo. I told her, "Shelly, look, Vermont is freezing in February. Why do you think I moved to California?" Never mind, before we left she rented *The Shining* again and is gunning for something "inbred and weird" happening to us. Tortured New England psychos, Shelly goes for that, but when we finally got to our rented condo in our rented vehicle and unpacked our rented skis and made standard, army issue love on our spongy, rented bed, well, even Shelly had to admit the probability of a supernatural occurrence seemed long.

So I'm spending the day loitering around town shopping while Shelly skis. Rich filth, that's me. Or at least what the man behind the cash register sees. What does he see? An expensive example of moral decay, of shit, and you know what? He's probably right. I've been living in Los Angeles for so long, the only things I do with much expertise are drive, fuck, shop, and rewrite murder mystery scripts. I'm referred to as a "comer" in the industry if you can fucking believe that. As for skiing, they *make* more snow in California than falls to earth here. In fact, I refuse to ski on these slopes. They're nothing but black rocks on ice with a twister of tree root. The sky reminds me of a lovesick homosexual on a North Sea ferry about to take a dive.

The trinket shop I'm in has a feeling of simulated local production not unlike a Hollywood set. They would like you to believe they actually make things here, quilts and the rest of it, but they don't. Not anymore. There's a tinkling doorbell that make me want to urinate, just whip it out and piss on the postcards of deep powder skiing and row after row of maple syrup. Those tin cans of maple syrup, oooh, they get me with that hateful illustration of a New England harvester bent before a pail that is in turn attached to a . . . a . . . is that what a maple tree really looks like? Since I'm the only person in the store, the owner and I have built up an unspoken animosity I'm savoring.

I finally remember why I'm here. I need a lighter. Turns out they're next to the camping pocketknives. I unfold the main blade and test its sharpness on my thumbnail. It's the kind of knife I hate. I scrape the lettering off a red "Killington" lighter and by the time I get to the counter, the thing reads, "Kill." I have plenty of cash in my pocket, but I plop down an American Express Platinum card.

"Charge it," I say.

"I've already called the police," says the man.

"Excuse me?"

"Vandalizing my merchandise is against the law."

"I'm buying your merchandise."

"We don't accept American Express."

I reach into my Willie Bogner ski suit purchased at great expense exclusively for this trip and take out a fat wad of cash.

"Fine, here's three hundred dollars."

"I don't want your money."

"Four hundred dollars."

"People like you should stay off the slopes."

So something supernatural is going to happen after all. Here come the Killington police.

Ten minutes later I'm on the street with a free lighter and pocketknife shooting the shit with these extremely chatty police officers. They have a grudge against the store owner, who they say is consistently late with his rent and wastes their time on calls like this one. They cradle my California driver's license, twisting it in the fading light so that it shimmers and shakes in high-tech lamination. They speak with awe of the efficiency of the LAPD computers. Do I need a ride somewhere? Yes, as a matter of fact I do.

The Lederhosen is an après-ski bar. It is crowded and hot. As in a monster movie, people lumber about in unbuckled ski boots, frozen grins plastered to their New England mugs. Shelly, I'm proud to announce, is easily the best-looking woman in the bar. She's going with the Edie Sedgwick–

Jackie O–Holly Golightly look. It's all in the hair band. She's wearing tortoiseshell shades, navy stretch pants, and an Alpine sweater, all part of her mythic East Coast iconography conceived from reading too much Truman Capote and watching rented videocassettes in Topanga Canyon. She's got a steaming mug in her hand, no doubt a hot toddy, and she's talking to a short man with a blown-out blood vessel for a nose and a face the color of a raw steak.

"Do you know what this gentleman said to me?" says Shelly as I smooch her on the cheek.

"What's that?"

"Listen to this. When I said, 'Single,' in the lift line, this guy who's buying us drinks, he comes right up to me, shakes my mitten, and says, 'Hi, my name's something-or-other, something-or-other.' Then he looks me right in the eye and goes, 'You want to hump?' He works for Wang Computers. He's been following me."

"Really," I say. "How's Wang doing?"

"We're relocating."

"I should think so, Lowell is a hole."

"Lowell *is* a hole, you wouldn't even know."

"No, I know. I've been there."

"Really?"

"Yes, I wonder why you haven't been laid off."

"Wise guy," says Mr. Wang. "Did you know that, Shell, you married a wise guy. How much did that snowsuit cost you there, wise guy?"

"After taxes probably what you pull down in a quarter. They tax the shit out of you in Massachusetts."

"This they do. What are you drinking there, wise guy, I'm buying."

"Whatever you're drinking."

"Seven and Seven."

I hate Scotch, but now I'm glad to have one in my hand. It's inspiring me to humiliate this man. Mr. Wang is extremely short, even in ski boots. He's practically a midget but confidently bundled in his bulky frame. He doesn't look stupid, just dangerously convinced of his right to be an asshole.

"Your wife wouldn't let me take her into the woods so on the lift I warmed my fingers up in her pie. You want to smell it?"

"Men know nothing about stretch pants," says Shelly. "These things are so tight you couldn't fit a nail file . . ."

"You want to smell it? Come here, wise guy. Smell it."

"Fuck you."

"OK, boys, it's time to go," says Shelly, standing up between us. Shelly takes my arm and we begin to walk. Events have unfolded so quickly, my anger hasn't had time to catch up with this hasty exit.

"See you tomorrow, Shell," says Mr. Wang. "Same lift line, OK?"

I feel for the camping knife in my breast pocket.

"I'll tell you what, buddy. I see you within a hundred meters of my wife and I'm going to stick you, man. I'm going to cut you up like a pig."

"A metric type, are we? He doesn't look like much of a skier, Shell. If I were you, I'd reconsider. It's never too early to trade up."

Outside the Lederhosen Mr. Wang is framed in the window. He's looking directly at me sniffing his finger and smiling.

The next day we ski in silence. There's just enough ice to hide the rocks, and every time the chair lift grinds to a halt and we're left hanging in the wind, I imagine it is Mr. Wang who has delayed us from below.

"Let's kill him," I say.

"I could be down with that," says Shelly.

"I'm serious."

"Fine, let's do him."

"I love you, sweetie," I say. "I love your guts."

I am reminded of Shelly's criminal youth spent in Topanga Canyon, her forced entry and burglary of Don Henley's house, her obsession with Sadie, the Manson chick who stabbed Sharon Tate. We have a joke about Sadie. According to *Helter Skelter,* a book we both admire, Sadie announced to the room as she was sticking Sharon, she stated that it took "a lot of love" to gore a movie star.

"He's a pig," says Shelly.

"Yeah, and it's going to take a lot of love," I say.

"A pig. No one could possibly miss him, not even at Wang."

We both laugh nervously. Neither of us have killed anyone, but we've gotten to the point in our lives where we'd like to see some people dead. Plus since I'm a script fixer for the television and film industry I've rewritten three hundred and seventy-eight murders as of last count on my computer.

Then there's this honeymoon. Nothing seems to separate it from a really bad vacation. The snow is terrible, the people insular and rude, the food fattening.

That night we retreat in lovey-dovey seclusion to our condo. Once we get the gas fireplace torching the logs, we can't find the wine opener so the corks are pushed in. I roll a joint with the skin of a Cuban cigar. We play backgammon and strategies. The pitch goes something like this. OK, rich Hollywood couple flies out to the East Coast to get away from the glitter. They meet an extremely unsympathetic character who insults their pride and honor. After dinner, I bend Shelly over and raid every orifice. I can't even count her orgasms. Bang, more wine, and back to the backgammon table. Shelly has the ability, when animated, to do five things at once. She's drinking wine, playing backgammon, smoking pot, listening to music, and drawing a hateful charcoal portrait of our mark. It's entitled "Sticking Mr. Wang." She's just finished Gide's *Adventures of Lafcadio,* the book about a motiveless murder, and this is making her paranoid. Since witnesses overheard my threats at the Lederhosen, my motive has been established. I counter. Yes, some skiers may have heard my threat, but Mr. Wang was alone, and come to think of it, could there not be a better place to get rid of someone than the anonymity of a ski slope? It's so cold half the skiers are wearing masks. The Killington brochure boasts thousands upon thousands of tourists a year. We've never used a credit card in the Lederhosen. No one knows our last name except the condo and ski rental people. The fact is this is an extremely artificial community in a constant state of flux.

"That's true," says Shelly. "They'll probably pin it on a snowboarder. We could make it look like a robbery."

"Let's get him in the woods," I say.

"It's supposed to snow tomorrow."

We turn on the Weather Channel.

"Look," says Shelly, flipping through the *TV Guide*. "We just missed *Murder, She Wrote.*"

Oh my God, what hilarity. We're both rolling around on our wall-to-wall carpet getting off on how thrilling it would be to sodomize Angela Lansbury and then slit her throat.

"I want you to cut him, honey," says Shelly, banging my head on the rug so I see stars. "Stick it in, move it up and twist. Make him die from the inside, you know what I'm saying? Don't go after his throat, that could get messy. Make him die from the inside."

"I'm going to have to be high as hell," I say, kissing her. "Stoned."

"Don't worry," says Shelly. "I'll get you high."

That night Shelly doesn't use her diaphragm for the first time in years. This is our honeymoon after all, and we're gunning for an infant.

So I'm in the woods playing with my pocketknife. All these other tools are a distraction. The scissors, nail file, can opener, toothpick, each drains away the efficacy of the blade itself. Perhaps I should use the saw. The saw looks good. I've been smoking grass for breakfast and lunch. Some people say the drug mellows you out, but I've never seen it that way. It's always made me conspiratorial and dangerous and today is no different. I'm wearing red-tinted goggles for energy and a suede ski mask. Also I'm glad that my burgundy Bogner suit has a slippery satin-like quality that won't absorb blood easily. Shelly and I have synchronized our Tiffany watches to California time. It's been threatening to snow all day but so far it hasn't. I have no idea what kind of trees are in these woods. Perhaps they are pines.

Earlier this morning we sat and drank coffee, smoked dope, and got real about this killing. The view from our condo offered a parking lot and the main lift-ticket line in the distance. We spent all morning with my Nikon binoculars taking turns searching for Mr. Wang.

"Did you see what kind of lift ticket he bought?" I ask.

"I don't know, but he said he was leaving tomorrow."

"That could have been a line. You know, establish a short timetable so as to hurry things up."

Shelly spots him getting out of a Subaru.

"Go," she says. "I'll see you in the woods, and remember, honey, wait until he's fucking me."

"Marriage is murder," I say, giving her a kiss goodbye.

"Murder if you fuck it up," she says.

So here I am, and I'll tell you it was a joyless morning of solo skiing. Everywhere I looked I saw crosses, white crosses on red. They're not even hot skiers, the ski patrol, just competent, bland guys. Luckily the conditions are so bad, people are hurting themselves. The ski patrol is busy either planting orange flags near rocky patches or carrying invisible victims downhill in toboggans.

Here comes Mr. Wang a few minutes early. I keep my head down. Shelly has given explicit instructions. She's put on her special "trapdoor" long underwear. She'll make sure he's on top. Myself, I've never been one for performing in the great outdoors, and in this weather, my concern has been Mr. Wang's ability to get it up. It was not a worry Shelly shared with me during our planning.

"Just take care of the knife, honey."

Two past eleven, LA time. Here comes my baby. She's sliding gracefully between the trees, really beaming. Mr. Wang stands to greet her, and they slide into each other's arms. Now Shelly leads him deeper into the woods to my left. She shakes her hair out of her ski hat and goes to work. I'm not supposed to watch. I've been instructed to "keep Tiffany time" and look out for courageous tree skiers. If one comes, the show is off. I do what I'm told. I allow two and a half minutes for foreplay, another minute and a half for clothing complications, another miscellaneous minute, only then am I to move. Time's up. I raise my head. Mr. Wang has a flask out. They're drinking! Oh my God, what's going to happen to my timetable? I move laterally in order to achieve a straight downhill position. This proves difficult and extremely annoying. My ski boots break the crust, and I keep sinking down to my knees. Each step is a nightmare. In fact, by the time I'm in position, I'm gasping for air, sweating through my long underwear and experiencing a disturbing deflation of motivation. Shelly on the other hand has begun to act out her end with such convincing aplomb, I'm beginning to wonder. There goes the "trapdoor." Mr. Wang drops his ski pants. He's got a fat ass in red long johns. Now he's on top of my wife. As I expected, however, no grinding. It's been too much, Shelly too aggressive, the woods awkward, the temperature nonconducive. Shelly responds to Mr. Wang's limpness by propping him up on his knees. Mr. Wang's navy parka blocks my view. No matter, if a tree falls in the woods, it still happened. I don't need to see shit to know exactly what Mr. Wang is feeling. Shelly's suction is tremendous, her technique exemplary. But there is something about Mr. Wang's inability to get it up that has lent him a place in my heart. Of course, Shelly is too much for him. Male fallibility, it strikes a chord and links us all in a great chain of misconduct.

Still, I've never seen Shelly work it like this. Three and a half straight minutes is a long time to suck a man's dick. Finally she grabs his neck and whispers in his ear. There goes the "trapdoor" again. Finally his ass begins to pump, but I don't want to kill this guy. I don't, but to break from our preplanned synchronization would be a betrayal Shelly would certainly make me pay dearly for. After all, she's done her part, performed her function. Now it's my time. I begin my downhill march, cursing myself for not renting cross-country skis.

Shelly has always lived beyond me. As for our offspring, I've often speculated upon their genetic code. They will fly or they will fall. My camping knife is raised, and I'm looking my wife in the eye. I decide to let him fuck her, to let him finish it, let him come, and so for a moment in time one could never measure, I watch. Then in a great underhanded swoop, I stick the knife up his ass and leave it there.

Back in sunny LA. We joke about "going about our daily routine as if nothing has happened," but Shelly being Shelly remains silently disappointed in me. She's looked into the statute of limitations on an out-of-state aggravated assault charge. I counter that she knows nothing about New Englanders. They are congenitally guilty people. Shelly says she's waiting for the "knock on the door." Paranoid bullshit, I tell her. Mr. Wang will suffer a humiliating visit to the doctor's office and perhaps a permanent case of hemorrhoidal flare. That's it. The punishment has fit the crime. He will *not* come after us. Shelly disagrees, but in her tempestuous bitchiness, which lasts well into her second trimester, I sense a hidden motive.

As for me, I'm plagued by my own paranoid vision. As we packed to leave the condo that night, I noticed Shelly's diaphragm lying upended on the toilet. It sat there so still, so definitively *un*inserted that I held it up on three fingers, a chalice to our folly.

My assistant Jane thinks I'm self-destructing. I've recently been promoted to a new office on the lot, and they've given me a budget for redecorating. Jane thinks I should go for the faux-Quaker-sparse look, a few spindly chairs and a laptop, the Zen thing. But it's like fuck Hollywood. I refuse not only to move from my old office but to redecorate the new one, a sure sign of insanity, Jane assures me. Sure she's talked to her shrink about it, and she isn't afraid to tell me exactly what they've discussed. After all, she rises as I rise, falls as I fall.

I dream of Mr. Wang. He is a smaller version of his already small self screaming the names of hateful Massachusetts towns: Chelmsford, Tewksbury, Dedham, Natick, Billerica. I am forced to drive him to all of them. But he does not actually want to visit them. Instead he is content to see their exit signs on the highway and move on.

I fear my wife. We fight. Our sex declines. As the baby grows and grows, I am seized with a premature ejaculation problem I haven't suffered since college. Shelly is left hanging. Imagine leaving Shelly hanging, bad news for any marriage, but Shelly is especially cruel about it. She speaks of buying a vibrator. Plus, the pregnancy is making her crazy. She insists on planning, planning, planning. She buys me a "baby beeper" to which only she knows the number. It's a boy. It's normal. It's my job to shop for his crib, toys, etc. The color is blue. Because the trades have announced my upward mobility in the industry, various Los Angeles sluts want to fuck me. I buy them drinks and take to degrading them in West Hollywood motel rooms. Sad part is this cheap sex is haunted because as I rise for the money shot, I am visited by an evil essence—that of a red baby, a demon, a monster. Matter of fact, this amazing girl half my age wants it really badly in the ass, when my beeper sounds. What to do? I keep fucking her, but afterward not only is there the usual comedown, but I realize I have a long and tedious drive to witness the immaculate delivery of Mr. Wang's baby.

Reggae Nights

He was pissing next to his golf cart with an exquisitely fine rum drink in one hand. Before him lay the beach. Alex was trying to settle in to his vacation but so far he'd just been drinking. Two and a half weeks of vacation was all he got at his new job and what with the market plunging on the day of his departure and then missing the connection from Miami due to Vivian's sunglass shopping, after all that, he'd taken to calculating percentage of vacation wasted in transit. It was double the yield on a fucking thirty-year treasury note, for Christ's sake.

Alex zipped himself up and watched as birds dove for prey into the Gulf Stream. It was two days after Christmas, and the tropical storm that had curled up from South America was well out to sea, making for a forest fire of a sundown. It reminded Alex of his former law firm. They'd had great sunsets from the twenty-third floor on Maiden Lane, just gorgeous, even if they were framed evening after evening within the modest window of a middling associate's office. Alex used to practice law, and though it was a grind, at least he had the comfort of being on an extremely expensive clock. There was no money to be lost, really. It was quite a contrast from his new nail-biting job glued to a Reuters trading screen in a windowless midtown hedge fund office. Now after nineteen straight months of currency speculation, he was finally on vacation, and what was he doing? Worrying about the weak yen while walking on a wonderfully beautiful beach. This was the first time Alex had been alone, really alone, i.e. not on the treadmill alone, but solo, utterly by himself, in months.

The beach was the color of chalk with a sprinkling of pink coral, and the storm had kicked up some aquamarine Bahamian surf that excited him. Alex took off his pants and shirt, and in a telltale sign of drunkenness, folded them neatly on the beach. Then he dove in. It was as warm as the baths his mother used to draw for him, warm and frothy and quite shallow. On the crest of a wave he stuck out his chest and cut sideways with the break all the while picturing Vivian on the beach watching him. As he waded out to catch another wave, there came a sailboat sideslipping across the surf. It ran aground a few yards from the beach. Someone had pulled up the centerboard, and a loose halyard line clanked noisily against the mast. Alex swam out to have a look at its stern. The boat was called *Troubadour II.*

He rode another wave and then walked down the beach in his boxers with his drink. It was called a Yellow Bird, and they were fucking delicious. He hoisted himself up on the gunnel and peered in. Blood mixed with seawater sloshed about in a baby blue cockpit, and wrapped in a spinnaker sheet was a black man. He'd been shot through the stomach and was gasping for breath and bleeding through his nose and mouth.

"Fuck," said Alex.

The dying man locked his eyes on Alex and then slowly raised his hand toward a hopeless expanse of ocean. He was trying to say something, but the effort was clearly going to kill him.

"Shhh," said Alex. "Shhh. I'm going to give you CPR. Don't die, OK? It's going to be fine. Just don't fucking die."

But the man was going . . . going and by the time Alex had climbed aboard, he was gone.

Alex's first impulse was to run for help. Certainly he needed assistance, but of what kind he was not sure. He pictured the island's harbor master, a huge beefy man with nautical patches on his shoulders walking up and down the docks with a whistle in his mouth. He didn't need that. As Alex moved to close the dead man's eyes, he stubbed his toe on the centerboard and fell against the body. The boat was tilted so that every step was a miasmic agony of strange gravity. The main cabin door was flung open, and Alex peered in. A tepid light filtered through the low Plexiglas ceiling, and besides being cramped and hot, the place stank of brine and sweat, of salt water cut with blood and urine. A baseball cap sat on top one of three bales of marijuana. Alex put on the hat and was surprised to find it fit perfectly. The idea behind the hat was it was supposed to help him think clearly; instead the hat served to disengage himself further from his actions, and in his mind's eye he rose to watch his meager little body stumble about the boat.

"What we have here," said Alex suddenly, needing to hear his own voice, "is a great drug miscommunication."

He gazed out at the ocean. A motorboat, possibly a Boston Whaler, partially eclipsed the sundown, and its outboard motor whined terribly in the distance. It was headed straight for the *Troubadour II*. Alex embraced a bale of marijuana in the shape of the world's largest Tootsie Roll. Overestimating the bale's weight, he hit his head on the ceiling. The bale was wrapped in a twine that scratched his forearms, and for a moment he paused in the tilted cockpit, cradling the pot as if it were a child. He had never touched marijuana in a quantity larger than the zip-locked bag variety and that had been years ago in college. It wasn't as if he coveted the bale; instead he desired participation in a drama. Clearly the man had gotten dead over drugs, and for some inexplicable reason Alex wanted a sliver of the action, a souvenir of the slaughter. A crafty feeling of marauding stealth came over him as the sound of what was now clearly a Boston Whaler grew in strength. The Whaler was evil. The Whaler was death and its approach threw him into a panic of impending persecution. Cautiously he eased himself from the stern of the *Troubadour II* and headed for shore. Still in his boxers, he loaded the bale into the golf cart and took off down the road.

Beneath blue bottles stuck in the fish netting and across from grinning photographs of big-game fishermen holding up fodder for the local taxidermist sat Tom Berman and Vivian Tate. They were discussing high school reunions over rum drinks and conch fritters. Vivian was an extremely pretty, precocious investment banker in a stage of intoxication when the will to narrate has begun to outweigh the capacity to listen. She was not a shallow woman, it was just that the shimmering monetary surface of things had come to envelop her inner life. She hadn't read a novel since business school, and increasingly a set of rather mercenary financial considerations informed her love life. Tom Berman was a college friend of Alex's. He'd met Vivian a few times at parties, but they'd never talked much. Tom worked as an enforcement attorney for the Securities and Exchange Commission. As a rule, Vivian didn't like government regulators, and as a rule Tom thought investment bankers scum. But this investment banker was such gorgeous scum that his feeling for her was one of perfectly intertwined spite and attraction. They knew better than to talk business with each other.

"Prize for the greatest tenth reunion alteration goes to John Goldstein," said Tom. "The guy was the upper-school drug dealer. So I walked up to him to see how he was doing, and it's like this wall of Yiddish I'd forgotten was flung in my face. He's currently attending the Rabbinical Studies program at Johns Hopkins. Everyone else was almost exactly the same. I thought they'd been embalmed or something."

Vivian sipped her drink. She was not impressed. It wasn't as if she would never marry a Jew, but with men she often made pros and cons columns, and though religion was never weighted very heavily in the scheme of her romantic asset allocation program, an outspoken Jew was not in the pro column.

"That's funny, because our brightest religious star had fallen from her cross," replied Vivian. "I mean, she was a true believer, Amy Colt. I'd imagined she'd be working with street kids in São Paulo or something. Wrong. She turned into a local TV personality in Delaware."

"What does she cover?"

"I don't know. The races . . . Hey, look who finally washed up. We were going to order without you," said Vivian. "I was thinking of going with the conch burger followed by the conch chowder, but you were so late, we already ate the conch fritters."

"Nice hat," said Tom. "Where'd you get it?"

"Off a bale of dope," said Alex, gripping the back of a chair. "What are you guys drinking? Whatever it is, I want a triple. Hey, excuse me, hey, could I get a drink, please."

"We're doing their 151 punch," said Vivian. "You could fry a conch fritter on top of it if anyone had a match. Do you have a cigarette, Alex? I'm having a low-grade nic fit."

"Excuse me, could I get a drink, please," shouted Alex.

But he might as well have been masturbating. The sound of frying foods cackled in the background, and the waitress was talking to the cook who was in turn watching a stock car race on ESPN. A Bahamian child with an Orlando Magic tank top was the only being moving. He raced around the restaurant playing tag with himself. The feeling was that of total island complacency. The restaurant might as well have been the waitress' living room rather than her place of business, and since Vivian and Tom were her only customers, there was an added incentive not to move. He would have to force contact. He walked up to the woman and asked her for a rum punch. She eyed him with sleepy suspicion, stabbed out a cigarette, and waddled over to the bar.

"A 151 punch, please," said Alex.

"What is your rush, young man? We are all sinners in the eyes of the Lord."

Ah, a preacher's daughter or perhaps the wife of a preacher. Alex, not desiring to embark upon an epistemological discussion, backtracked.

"I'm sorry to hurry you, ma'am, but it's been a pretty harrowing evening so far."

She gave him his drink, and he sat down next to Vivian. Since their fateful business trip to Washington, they'd slept together a dozen times, work schedule permitting. They did, they really did try to "fit one another in," but they were mutually suspicious lovers. Vivian was searching hard for a husband, and it was certainly not going to be Alex. She might have considered him if he had stuck to the law, but since consistency and "earning power" were character traits she admired in a potential mate, Alex was off the list. But if Alex were off the list, why then was she on this vacation? Since she was twenty-eight years old, this was certainly not the time to dally in short-term lust operations. She wanted to make a rich team with her husband and live a life of compounded wealth with multiple domiciles in and out of the continental United States. But instead, she was on this rather rundown, miserable little island with a man who showed no great aptitude for high finance and who on top of it all had shot her in the leg. The fact was they had rarely gone anywhere together as a couple except the Harvard Club, where Vivian had to pay the room bill for their lunch-hour sex.

"So what's this noise about dope?" asked Tom.

"Now, why would I want to inform the federal government about a crime in motion?" said Alex.

"Hey, man, why do you think I didn't want to go to South Beach," replied Tom. "You know what was at the top of my vacation action item list?"

"What?" asked Vivian, who'd made an action item list herself.

"Jurisdiction," said Tom. "Non-U.S."

Suddenly Alex was finding it difficult to indulge in vacation badinage. His rum drink seared his stomach lining, and in his mind's eye he returned to the dying man wrapped in the bloody spinnaker sheet pointing out to sea, pointing like the "Touch of God" out to sea. The last half hour of Alex's life had not, it turned out, been a sequence in a high-budget adventure dream starring himself truly. Plus, he'd left his pants, shoes, and wallet on the beach for the guys in the Whaler to find. Suddenly, he felt he was going to be sick and rushed outside to vomit. Through the prism of his tears, he looked sideways to see Tom and Vivian laughing in the street. They were backlit by a low-wattage Bahamian street lamp. The Yellow Birds so smooth in going down were coming up in great torrents of acid that scalded his esophagus. Suddenly, he was visited by a great sexual ambivalence toward Vivian. Bent over, he saw only her golden shoes. They appeared aggressively fashionable in the context of this island, hopelessly urbane. No doubt they were Italian and expensive. They were perpendicular to one another in a third-position ballet turn-out she usually reserved for cocktail parties. He hated them, but he wanted to touch them too. He wanted to buy every single pair of those shoes sold on the island of Manhattan and present them to Vivian at her funeral.

"You OK there, bud?" asked Tom, patting his friend on the back.

"No," said Alex. "I left my clothes and wallet on the beach. I had to go back to the Sea Breeze and change. They're going to come after us."

"I see," said Tom. "So what you're saying is you have a streaking problem."

"Look, Tom," said Alex. "Can we pay for our drinks at this place and keep moving. Our best bet for this evening is a hit-and-run kind of operation. Could you go in there and pay the lady?"

It was a wonderfully breezy evening, and they drove around the island on the golf cart hitting potholes and spilling rum drinks on one another. Between his friend and lover in the singing electricity of the cart, Alex felt safe and vaguely heroic telling his tale. Clouds slipping beneath the moon were briefly illuminated, and then gone. Vivian was in a state of rapture. This was better than all the New York wedding gossip lined up in a row, and she kept up a running inquiry that made no bones about the levity she found in the calamity.

"And it's pretty sick too, you taking the baseball cap," she said. "I might be able to take this a little more seriously if you hadn't taken the cap."

But she refused to take the cap off her head. It was white with a red letter "B" for Bahamas.

"Maybe we should dye your hair," said Vivian. "I brought

some henna a nymphomaniac friend of mine brought back from Turkey. I think we should dye your hair."

"Maybe I should *shave* my head," said Alex.

"Maybe you should tell me where you hid the drugs," said Tom.

"Why, so the Feds can confiscate it?"

"He's got a good point there," said Vivian. "What we need here is plausible deniability for you, Tom."

"Fuck you two," said Tom. "Fuck you both. I'm serious. I don't need this shit on vacation."

Tom was driving, and if the truth be known he was torn. He had badly needed a break from monitoring trades, Chinese food, and incessant paperwork. Unlike Alex, Tom was relieved to be cut free from work, and it wasn't as if he had a hard-on for the DEA either. Drugs had never been his department. His specialty was analyzing trades in targeted takeover companies in the weeks prior to a merger announcement. The risk arbitrage people feared him. He had nothing to do with drugs because he had a history with them, latent though it was. Now, set free on a foreign island with several drinks in him, Tom Berman, a sworn member of the Securities and Exchange Commission, wanted to get high.

"Seriously, Alex, where'd you hide it?"

"Take a left," said Alex.

Off Queens Way Road and in the tepid headlights of the golf cart they arrived at a church. It was a modern structure with reinforced concrete beams and huge, darkly tinted windows. In back was a graveyard. As the trio entered, Alex prayed for cloud cover. He felt naked and watched in the moonlight, certain that it was only a matter of time before the men in the Whaler tracked him down and cut his face to shreds.

"You are a morbid man," whispered Vivian in Alex's ear. "A morbid man. I don't know why I have anything to do with you."

"All I know," said Tom, "is that I'm not in the office."

"Is that a good thing or a bad thing?" asked Vivian.

"I have yet to find that out."

The earth beneath them was spongy from the rains. These were shallow graves, and to Alex, the field felt alive with an awful subterranean activity.

"This is like that scene in *The Good, the Bad and the Ugly*," said Vivian. "You know, three gunslingers in a graveyard looking for gold."

"Would you shut up," said Alex.

Tom lit the flashlight he'd taken from the back of the golf cart. There it was, two graves over, plump and tasty, ready for the taking.

"Maybe it's an Oreo," said Tom. "I hope to fucking God it's an Oreo."

"What the hell is an Oreo?" asked Alex.

Vivian knelt before the bale, but Tom, taking over drug command central, pushed her over onto the ground.

"Take it back," she said. "This is more like *Charlie's Angels* takes over the set of *Live and Let Die*. I'm waiting for Mr. Big."

Someone had once given Vivian a line of coke at the Speed Club, and she hadn't done drugs ever since. She wasn't interested in them. She liked her wine and her vodka tonics. Why boys sought out drugs had always mystified her. Alex watched as his friend's forearm disappeared into the middle of the bale. It came out holding a zip-locked bag of cocaine.

"Bingo," said Tom. "We got an Oreo. The sweet spot's in the middle. These days it behooves no one to move grass alone. It's simply not cost effective."

Tom opened up the bag and pulled out a handful. Then he stuck his nose in the pile.

"Jesus," said Vivian. "We'd better get out of here."

"A virtually uncut Oreo at that," said Tom, passing his hand beneath Alex's waiting nose.

"Boys," said Vivian, standing up. "Boys, I don't mind being an accessory to a crime. What I don't appreciate is folly."

"Shut up," said Tom. "I'm on vacation."

"You're doing coke in a graveyard."

Suddenly the moon broke through the clouds, casting the trio in its quicksilver.

"She's right," said Alex. "Let's disappear."

Back at the Sea Breeze a man named William Hunter, better known on the island as Devil, had Vivian's toothbrush stuck up his ass, head first. He and his crew, high as hell, had just about finished robbing the bungalow. Now they were leaving their signature calling card. Devil's brother James was known as Lucif. He was taking a photograph of his brother's ass with Alex's Nikon. Both men were standing on adjoining beds laughing. The Sea Breeze was the farthest bungalow from the main office and was easily accessible from the beach. Not bad, thought Devil of his surroundings. This was a fine fuck house if he did say so himself, a fine fuck house.

"Don't let me see your face, Devil," said Lucif. "That's good, that's good. Now, shake that pink handle, shake it, shake it hard."

Lucif put the camera on high speed drive and rattled off the rest of the roll. Then the brothers stepped off the beds and returned to their drinks and a smoldering joint left in the living room ashtray. "Cones" is what they called their joints. Devil was the master roller. He was a Haitian whose flotilla bound for Miami had broken up in the Bahamas three years ago. The third man was a local short-order cook named Leslie Hibert. Besides his fondness for zip guns, Leslie had a wife who was a maid. The wife wasn't so much a thief as a provider of information to thieves. The two brothers thought their partner something of an amateur, and while out on jobs they liked to smoke their cones and degrade him. Still they needed Leslie. His wife had a passkey to over half the resort rooms on the island.

Naturally the trio enjoyed reggae music, and instead of simply robbing the Sea Breeze and leaving as was their custom, tonight they played a little chicken with the gods of crime. It was a Friday night and each man settled into his perch in the living room as Devil turned on the stereo. He'd put on "The Harder They Come," something of a corny golden oldie, he had to admit, but still a breakthrough record nonetheless. Devil had once been a bassist in a band called Loose Caboose. They'd played the island circuit for two and a half years before splitting up over money and internal differences concerning Rastafarian iconography. Currently he was in a band that was into more of an island rapping scene. He was thieving in order to get up enough cash for a trip to Nassau, where he planned to buy two turntables and a bass amplifier. He badly wanted to scratch and sample like the guys on Yo-MTV. Devil was keeping up with the times. He saw himself as something of a reformed reggae burnout turned gangster.

Secretly Devil was impressed with the music selection. Besides the obvious tourist's stuff like Marley, there was some serious old school by Sun Ra, the Maytals, Desmond Dekker, and even the Slickers. In short Devil and his crew had never robbed a tourist shack with better taste in reggae. It was time to light up. Besides, it was early yet and Leslie's wife had said from the looks of things, these tourists would probably be out dancing to the steel drum band at Mr. Beckford's. From where Devil sat, they had at least another hour to kick it in.

"Devil, you going to pass me that cone," said Lucif, "or am I going to have to climb up from this couch and kick your ass?"

Devil paid little heed to his brother's request. He sat there implacably stoned on the couch palming his bald head. He was enjoying "Johnny Too Bad" immensely.

A flashlight cut the darkness and zeroed in on Devil's eyes. Leslie ran across the living room, broke through a sliding screen door, and was gone. The brothers Lucifer sat still as a stone.

"Look, man," came a voice. "My only request is that nobody gets hurt, OK. We have your drugs. Let me repeat. We have your drugs. They're intact and we're going to hand them over to you in an orderly fucking fashion."

There was a long silence. "Johnny Too Bad" was coming to a close. "Walking down the road with a pistol in your waist, Johnny you're too bad . . ." Devil slowly rose to his feet. Wired tourists suffering from some kind of delusions. He'd seen it happen before but none of them had ever offered him drugs. Devil was still sorting through the geometry of the situation when Lucif switched on the lights.

Now if this wasn't a sight. Standing not five yards from him was this fine white girl in one of those fine looking-for-the-good-wood white girl getups holding what looked to be a key of coke like it was road kill. Some other clown was hugging a bale.

"How I know you didn't cut the shit up?" asked Devil.

"Because we don't have a knife," said Vivian.

Devil walked out onto the patio. Alex dropped the bale on the lawn and put his arm around Vivian.

"This your lady?" asked Devil.

Alex said nothing. He was trying to remember how to deliver a "spear-hand poke" to the throat, but he was wired, terrified, and utterly unprepared for combat. Vivian stepped forward and handed the zip-locked bag to Devil.

"You're missing about six lines, OK?" she announced.

Tom turned off his flashlight. He was standing near the bushes out of range of the patio lights. There was no way he was going to let these guys see his face.

"You can put about a half a gram down to carrying charges and everyone walks," said Tom from the darkness.

"Who the fuck are you?"

"Someone you're never going to see again."

Devil, who rarely cut the nail on his left pinkie for moments just like this, opened the bag and did a noseful.

"If you'd cut it, we'd kill you," said Lucif, brandishing one of the Sea Breeze's steak knives. Devil was glad to see his brother had gotten into the spirit of the proceedings.

"I see you found our stereo," said Alex.

Vivian flinched. She knew not what this boy was talking about.

"I tell you what," said Devil. "You let me take in a little of the white lady with your woman here and I'm gone."

"Fuck you," said Alex.

"Alex," said Vivian. "Alex, come on. Shut *up*, will you? I'll do a line with you, mister."

And so Devil had his way on the very bed where his brother had snapped the toothbrush photos, and it was good, man, it was good. He held her hands over her head and went for every hole. Then he and his brother cut out for the beach.

They walked down a narrow path shaded on both sides by the resort's landscaping artist, Devil with the coke, Lucif with the grass. When they came to the dune below the clubhouse, Devil looked out onto the ocean. The wind had died and the moon cut the sea into lines of sequins, and within these shimmering flashes of water he recognized the Bailey brothers' Whaler. Devil yanked his brother down to the sand.

"Bailey brothers," he hissed. "Looks like they coming to steal back what they lost and we found."

"I'll see you back home," said Lucif.

"Johnny, you're too bad," said Devil.

They split up. Devil hid himself in a waist-high honey-suckle bush off the path. He'd never seen the Bailey brothers in action. They were the most feared drug dealers on the island, and in deference to their reputation, he lay as flat as he possibly could with the coke hidden in his crotch.

He imagined them coming, a scalding stream of vengeful menace moving uphill in their anger. But soon Devil did not have to imagine because he could hear their murmurs, the steely click of switchblades locking into position, and the hurried footsteps padding up the garden path, making for the Sea Breeze, a riptide soon to carry the dead out to sea.

Pure
Slaughter
Value

We are an acute triangle of three, my family, and since death has thinned our ranks, we tend to attach ourselves to other people. For a good many years it was the McPhersons. I was in love with the whole family. You want to see good American looks pollinated and passed along? Witness Mrs. McPherson standing barefoot on her crabgrass lawn party circa 1975. She's got her daughter by her side. I'd rather not talk about the daughter. Mr. McPherson is fondling my mother. An affair at these close quarters is out of the question, so Mr. McPherson gets what he can at greetings and departures. The gravel driveway churns with new arrivals. A party is under way, but the band does not strike up. No band here, just the golden sounds of banter, cocktails, and flirtation. Soon Mother is not the only one dwarfed by Mr. McPherson's shadow rising to meet his guests. There are other couples to chortle over and squeeze. The medicine is being mixed. Bloody Marys and wine on Marimekko porch furniture. The sixties are a soft touch here. Thus the confusion in dress code. The ties are fat, the espadrilles healed, the riotous political and military upheavals of the year tempered by a new Christ-like asceticism of sandals and open linen shirts worn by emaciated men who have just taken up long-distance running.

I am not at the party, but I can hear it. I'm with Sam McPherson lining up a cardinal perched on my mother's birdfeeder.

"Peg it," says Sam.

My Daisy rests on the windowsill. The trick is to kill as many songbirds as possible. The window is not far from the glass sliding doors. It's about a twenty-foot diagonal from the birdfeeder. So far I've taken out two blue jays and something else, relatively big targets. Now I'm after more difficult game. This shooting gallery is not like the photographs I've seen of my dead father grinning and crouched before animals he has killed in Africa, but there is a similarity. We're both in it for the pure slaughter value. Sam's dead birds lie on the wooden porch twitching.

I pull the trigger. Suddenly all the birds vanish from the feeder. Nothing falls.

"Shit!" I say. "Fuck. Your mother sucks cocks in hell. Fuck."

I am eleven, a good swearing age. Sam is sixteen and heavily into obscenity too. He's taught me all my combinations.

"You worthless little piece of shit," he says, seizing the gun from my hands. A car comes up the driveway toward the party. Sam dings a BB off the side door. There's nothing he hates more than his parents' parties.

"I'm going to count to five," he says.

I was so fast back then it makes me want to cry. Off the porch, across the lawn, over Mrs. Warnicky's fence, into a slalom course of evasive tree moves inspired by various war movies, down to the bay, through the reeds, and back up to the party, where I take refuge behind my mother.

"What's the matter, Louis?"

I compose myself.

"Nothing," I say. "Nothing, just hacking around. You know."

"Sam's putting the fear of God into him again," says my mother's boyfriend, inspecting a welt on my arm. "I bet he's popping you with that Daisy, isn't he? Where is that thing? I want to take it out of that vandal's hands."

"Frank," I say, "you got any of those M-8os on you?"

"Later, Louis," he says. "It depends on this party."

Frank used to be in the Army, and he still has a green metal box of explosive goodies he likes to take out on special occasions. Now he works in the book business. Frank's M-8os have waterproof fuses. They blow up underwater and scare the shit out of the swans cruising Mecox Bay. Then there are the nuns. The M-8os are for the nuns too. The McPhersons' front lawn gives onto a view of a convent across the bay. Sometimes we can see the nuns walking on the convent lawn, their white wings barely visible on their heads.

The party is in full swing now, and the parents are making me into an ice hockey legend. It is the hour of expansiveness, of compliments, of sexual jousting. They are so inspired. The sun is just beginning to set and there is talk of the Greater New York City Ice Hockey League.

"He has to get up at six in the morning, to go out to that rink you pass on the way to La Guardia, just amazing," says my mother.

"How does he get there?" says Mrs. McPherson.

"I've got a grad student, but I'm a little worried he stays up all night before he drives Louis out."

"He probably does, but maybe that's better," says Mrs. McPherson. "Why so early?"

"You think the city can afford to rent out Madison Square Garden to the Pee-Wees?" says my mother.

"Mother," I say.

"It's sick," says my mother. "No city money whatsoever for this league . . ."

"Mother."

"What, honey?"

"I can tie my skates fine now."

When I was nine, I didn't have anyone around to tie my skates; so this man with a son on our team used to tie them for me. He'd fling the dregs of his coffee on the rubber floor, flip one of my skates into his fleshy paws, and sigh. These were not the first pair of skates he'd tied early that morning. A hockey dad, it was a pain in the ass, and he let me know just how tiresome it was by pulling hard and clamping his index finger down on the crossed laces, moving up my skate in a grunting muscular rhythm. Then I'd step out onto the ice, tears in my eyes, unable to feel my feet. Now it's no problem.

"That's great, Louis," says my mother. "Next season we're going to get you to those games on time even if I have to drive you myself."

"Nelly, please," says Mrs. McPherson to my mother. "At six in the morning on a Saturday? I don't think so."

"OK, OK," says my mother. "But I'm going to start going to more night games."

"Well, that's an improvement."

Sam McPherson walks into the equation. He's at an age of total parental loathing. He's nearly six feet tall, my best friend. He's gangly, bitter, and blond.

"How about we go upstairs, Louis?"

"Upstairs for what?" asks Sam's mother.

"None of your business, Mom."

Frank arrives smoking a cigar and carrying the olive green army box. This is a good sign. I've seen the look before. Time for a little gleeful adult destruction. The cigar amber is designed for the touching off of an M-80 fuse.

"Frank, no," cries my mother.

"Yes, Frank," I scream. *"Yes!"*

"All I can say," says Mrs. McPherson. "All I can say is I hope the nuns are sunbathing topless in Acapulco."

"Nelly, I want you to listen to the property owner here," says Frank. "I get the sense I'm getting clearance from the property owner, resistance from the renter."

The McPhersons own two houses. They live all summer in the big airy one, and they rent a smaller version to us on the far side of their back lawn. It's a happy arrangement.

"Now," says Frank.

I've got a sparkling M-80 in my hand and for a moment it's as if I'm staring at my hero, wowed by the burn-down.

"Now," says Frank. "Louis, now!"

I throw the M-80 into the bay. A thin geyser of water erupts, a fabulous discharge. The party cheers. I've tossed it so the M-80 hasn't had time to sink far enough to just rumble in the depths of the bay.

"That's enough, Frank," shouts Mrs. McPherson. "It was fun while it lasted, but the property owner is weighing in now. That's enough."

Frank closes his box, and we walk back up the lawn. He pats me on the back.

"Don't scare me like that, kid."

"What, Frank?"

"You know goddamned well what I'm talking about. A burning fuse is a burning fuse. It's not a romance. You got that?"

"Got it," I say.

But what do I know of romance? Ice hockey, Estes Rockets, bicycles, bodysurfing, BB guns, kick-the-can, baseball, canoeing, smear the queer, sailing, Monopoly, rock fights, these are my developed passions, my "skill set" as they say in the consulting business. But that being said, there is a movement afoot. My best friend is sixteen. He's already been thrown out of boarding school for taking an ax to a piano. Now he's waiting for me at the edge of the party, and he doesn't want to play kick-the-can.

We go upstairs via different routes at different times, not unlike lovers leaving a party in secrecy, at intervals. Upstairs is where we get it done with the pillows.

In thinking about the coming pillow fight, the requirement is to decouple the word "pillow" from the words "sleep," and "softness," from sky, from dreams, from cloud. The McPhersons' pillowcases are strong pouches of weathered cotton. Sam takes a long time packing his pillow. As he packs an iceball, so he decorates his weapon now, pressing down, down, holding the pillow as if he were pressing someone beneath a lake, really getting into it. The upstairs of the McPherson summer residence is not an attic but it has the low-ceilinged, panic-inspiring quality of an attic.

"So are you going to give me some time here, motherfuck?" I say.

"No time," says Sam, looking at his nonexistent wristwatch.

The sun runs through the window into my eye. Sam is coming in black and tall. His silhouette is that of a sinewy young athlete about to give up sports forever. He's taking the ball and chain approach right off. Usually he doesn't pack his pillow so tightly until I've scored at least a few blows.

"Just wait a fucking second," I say.

My sister comes to the doorway. She has a beer in her hand. She is fourteen. Never before have I seen my sister with an alcoholic beverage. She is tall, thin, beautiful, awkward. She's wearing jeans and a blue Indian print shirt bulging on her molehill breasts. She leans back to drink her beer, and for a moment I can see her belly button. My sister is in love with Sam, as I am in love with Sam's sister, Sarah. My sister and I are both terrified and thrilled by our love, but we have been unable to do anything but suffer longing. We feel the McPhersons are special, their house clearly haunted. My sister proved this to me one night when she invited me to a séance in Mrs. McPherson's bathroom. The only light was a candle. We sat cross-legged on the tiles mesmerized by the flame. The séances seal our superstition and secret pacts through the pouring of liquid wax.

"Give me your hand," she said, holding the candle ready. "If you hear an Elton John song within a minute, there is a ghost in the house."

"But Sam told me he was going to play 'Funeral for a Friend,' " I said.

I've caught her again, but I don't mind. She was so pretty, then, sitting on the tiles cooking the odds of love and superstition.

"Shhh, shhh," she said, her long brown hair curtaining her face. I reached for her hand and poured the wax. The pain meant nothing to her.

"Shhh, shhh," she said. "I love him."

"I love her."

"I know you do," she said. "But you're not old enough."

"Old enough for what?"

"You'll see."

My sister has seen these beatings before, and though I like to make a sport of getting on the other line when she's conversing with her male callers and yelling into the phone that she's flat, and though I generally love to monkey-wrench my sister's love life so that she reaches these great crescendos of homicidal rage, through all this, she does have sympathy when it comes to my uneven relationship with Sam.

"Oh shit," she says. "Not this again."

"Your mother sucks cocks in hell," says Sam. Now he has an audience, a witness to his beating. Sam likes that. But I like it too. My sister has always brought out the warrior in me. I pick my pillow and stuff it down. Let the games begin.

So I'm doing this little Ali routine—float like a butterfly sting like a bee—on the bed. The plan is to save the rope-a-dope for later rounds. I bounce on the springs. Then I'm on the floor and push the bed into the middle of the room. Now I've got something to run around. He clocks me on the head. I get him in the chest.

"Oh my God," says Sam. "I'm injured. I'm dying."

"The Rumble in the Jungle, jack," I scream. "The Thrilla in Manila motherfuck! You can't fucking touch me."

"Go, Louis," shouts my sister. "Get him."

"Your mother sucks cocks in hell."

Everyone's combinations are flowing tonight, but suddenly there is a variable, a third pillow. My sister has joined in. Everyone ends up on the bed. Now I'm rolling off; now Sam and my sister are laughing. What is this? These weaklings have left themselves open. I flagellate both of them, but they're laughing and loving the pain. The room is juiced with kicked-up dust in the sun, and the panic of the attic has receded from fight to frolic. No more rope-a-dope. I'm back to dancing, to flying, to inflicting damage on my sister and Sam wrestling on the bed.

"What the fuck is this, what the fuck is this?" I shout. "Spin the bottle? What the fuck is this?"

Sam gets up from the bed, stuffs his pillow back down,

and levels me. Then he says, "Louis, Louis, I want you to hyperventilate."

"What's that?"

"I want you to breathe and breathe. I want you to never stop breathing. Start sucking wind, now! In out, in out. Breathe. Like this."

I do what I'm told.

"More, keep breathing in and out, more, more breath."

I'm getting dizzy, and Sam has me by the throat. It tingles and then comes the rising feeling of anesthesia. I'm out. I have a split-second dream. I'm on a horse riding with Sam's sister, Sarah. I wake up. Sam and my sister are making out in the bed. The beer sits on the windowsill, and I walk over and pick it up. It is still cold.

Sarah is standing in the doorway, witnessing the first beer of my life. This room does not impress her. She's wearing her riding boots, and a saddle is slung over her shoulder. What's going on? Could I have caught a glimpse of Sarah before Sam passed me out? I love her. I love her diseased horse Fred stabled in a potato farm barn. Riding with her is the only thing she'll let me do, and she's only let me do it twice. When it's just me and Sarah and Fred, that's when I'm the happiest. It's even better than a rock fight with Sam. When I'm on Fred and have my arms wrapped around Sarah's waist, when we're running through the country and down the dune and out onto the beach, that's when I'm not sure if my tears come from the wind or from somewhere else.

"Let's go riding."

Acknowledgments

I would like to thank the following people for their support: Vanessa Chase and her mother Victory, Jay Mandel, Bruce Tracy, J. R. Walsh, Eoghan Mahony, Libby May, Laurie Adams, Deborah Garrison, Todd Jesdale, Amanda Gersh, William Mortan, and The Kid.